THEIRS EVER AFTER

A THALANIAN DYNASTY NOVEL

KATEE ROBERT

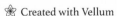 Created with Vellum

ALSO BY KATEE ROBERT

The Thalanian Dynasty Series (MMF)

Book 1: Theirs for the Night

Book 2: Forever Theirs

Book 3: Theirs Ever After

Book 4: Their Second Chance

The Kings Series

Book 1: The Last King

Book 2: The Fearless King

The Hidden Sins Series

Book 1: The Devil's Daughter

Book 2: The Hunting Grounds

Book 3: The Surviving Girls

The Make Me Series

Book 1: Make Me Want

Book 2: Make Me Crave

Book 3: Make Me Yours

Book 4: Make Me Need

The O'Malley Series

Book 1: The Marriage Contract

Book 2: The Wedding Pact

Book 3: An Indecent Proposal

Book 3.5: <u>Seducing Mr. Right</u>

<u>Other Books</u>

<u>Seducing the Bridesmaid</u>

<u>Meeting His Match</u>

<u>Prom Queen</u>

<u>The Siren's Curse</u>

1

"Not that way, Consort."

Meg Sanders veered to the right instead of the left in response to the whispered words. She'd officially been Consort to the King of Thalania for six months, and she still couldn't quite figure out the palace. It *should* be straightforward enough, but they never seemed to take the same path twice. Supposedly it had something to do with security and safety, but she couldn't shake the feeling that the staff here just flat out didn't like her.

"Consort." Another whisper behind her.

She bit back a sigh and raised her gaze to find none other than Noemi Huxley bearing down on her. Oh, Noemi was too perfect to *bear down* on anyone. She practically floated across the cool stone floors, her classic dress kicking out gently around her heels.

Meg had no illusions about her appearance—she was attractive and knew how to maximize that as needed—but Noemi made her feel about two feet tall and stunted without even trying. She had model-sharp cheekbones, a generous mouth, and honey blond hair that never seemed out of place. "Consort," she said with a smile and leaned in to press an air kiss to each of Meg's cheeks.

Another Thalanian custom that Meg would never get used to. It didn't matter that Thalania was far from the only European country that employed air kisses. She had a choice whether to accept them in other countries. As Consort, she was chained by a set of rules she still didn't have down pat. *No use thinking about that now. You made your choice.*

Yeah, she had.

She chose Theo.

And Galen.

Noemi stepped back, oblivious to the turmoil of Meg's thoughts and gave another warm smile. "I was hoping you had some time in your schedule in the next few days for tea. I feel like I haven't seen you in ages."

They had tea only last week, but Meg didn't have the heart to say it. It wasn't Noemi's fault that her every breath highlighted how perfectly she fit into life in the palace—and how the same couldn't be said for Meg. To her credit, Noemi never went out of her way to point that out. She was kind enough and seemed to genuinely want to spend time getting to know Meg. Which was more than Meg could say for most of the other noble Families.

Stop it. Focus. You can't afford to be distracted, even with Noemi.

Meg forced a smile of her own. "I'd like that a lot." She glanced over her shoulder at Alys, her own personal babysitter. The woman's official title was secretary, but they both knew the truth. "Alys, how does my schedule look tomorrow?" She didn't *think* there was anything, but she'd been wrong before.

Alys checked her ever-present tablet. "You're clear from two to three."

That's it? It took everything she had not to wilt at the words. Meg turned back to Noemi. "How does that sound?"

"Wonderful. I look forward to it." Noemi swooped down —at nearly six feet tall, she towered over Meg's five feet, seven inches—and pressed two more air kisses to her cheeks. "Have a good evening, Consort."

"You, too."

Meg resumed her course, careful to keep her chin up and her stride steady. God forbid she give into the urge to sprint through the halls to the relative safety of the private suite she shared with Galen and Theo. She followed Alys's quiet directions until they turned down a hallway Meg actually recognized. Bright, happy paintings clustered the walls, the sight of them making her smile despite herself. They had been acquired by Theo's mother years ago, right after she'd married his father and become Queen of Thalania. Theo had them moved to this hall the week after his coronation, a reminder of the woman who'd been so important to him.

Some days, Meg spent nearly an hour staring into the paintings, trying to reach back through time to the woman who'd picked them. They were such a random collection, their origins spanning multiple decades and many styles. The only real connection was the buoyancy in her chest when she allowed herself to spend time in this space. Did Theo's mother pick them because she was happy and wanted pieces to reflect that? Or were they her only bright spot in the stress that came from being with the most powerful man in Thalania?

The latter, Meg could relate to all too well.

She bit back a sigh and kept her spine straight as she

opened the door to the private suites. She paused and looked back at Alys. The woman had been a lifesaver for the last six months. Everything about her was just as understated as Noemi was glamorous. She tended to wear black with small pops of color—slacks and a blouse today—and the only jewelry Meg had ever seen on her person was a thin locket she wore around her neck. She never mentioned it and Meg didn't feel like it was her place to ask simply to satisfy her curiosity.

She managed a real smile. "We made it through the day."

"We did." Alys swiped her index finger across her tablet and pushed a few buttons. "I've sent over your agenda for tomorrow, along with any wardrobe considerations."

After a particularly brutal fashion mistake during her first solo social event, Alys had taken to giving her suggestions to help avoid it in the future. "Thanks. Have a good night, Alys."

"And you as well, Consort."

Meg shut the door and slumped against it. Once upon a time, she'd dreamed that a prince would ride into her small town and fall in love the moment he laid eyes on her. He'd rescue her from her shitty life, pull her astride his white horse, and they'd ride off into the sunset together.

That kind of thing only happened in fairy tales.

Meg had saved herself, had worked her ass off to get out of that hellhole of a town, had gotten into college, and was now one short year away from graduating with her Masters of Accounting.

Or she had been before she met that prince she'd given up waiting on to save her.

Turned out being a princess—or Consort—wasn't all she'd dreamed of.

In fact, it kind of sucked.

"Hey, baby."

She opened her eyes and turned to face the other man she loved—the one who occupied a second Consort position for the first time in Thalanian history. Galen Mikos. He hadn't bothered to turn on the lights in the sitting room, and he sprawled in the furthest chair from the door like some kind of dark god. She couldn't see his face clearly, but the exhaustion weighing her down was mirrored in the lines of his shoulders and thighs. "Hey." She stepped out of her heels and walked to him. "Long day."

"Yeah." He took her hand and pulled her onto his lap. Galen was built for war in the same way she imagined the Spartans had been—a heavy muscled and barely contained violence. When she met him in New York, that violence had been buried deep, only visible in a hint of a look when he let the mask drop. Here, it rode much closer to the surface. The fact he couldn't act on it in any real way just made the entire situation that much more complicated.

She pressed her face against his neck and inhaled his clove and tobacco scent. Meg had never seen Galen smoke, but he always smelled like he'd just got done rolling one of those clove cigarillos. "I spilled tea on Lady Nibley today. Right in her lap."

Galen shifted her closer and sifted his fingers through her hair, freeing the pins that had spent all day torturing her. "I sat through an entire meeting where Isaac fucking Kozlov talked to me like I was an idiot kid. He conveniently forgot that *I* was the one who trained him before he took over as head of security."

"I'm sorry." She kissed his jaw. "I know it wasn't supposed to be like this."

"No, it really wasn't." He cursed and tossed her hair pins onto the table near his feet. "You see Theo today?"

"Not since we all went our separate ways this morning." That was the other thing she hadn't bargained on. In hindsight, it made sense that Theo would spend all his waking hours in long meetings about everything from national security to concern over the drought putting half the country's crops in danger. Six months wasn't quite enough time to undo the damage his exile had caused, and as happily as the people had welcomed him back, his decision to name both Meg and Galen as Consort had made waves that would drown all three of them if they weren't careful.

It would help if Meg could stop fucking up.

Galen lifted his free hand and she knew without looking that he was checking his watch. "I've giving him an hour and then I'm going to track his ass down and haul him back here. He's running on empty."

"I know." She just didn't know how to fix it. The best Meg could do was try to ensure she wasn't a burden, but ever since coming to Thalania, that's exactly what she felt like. A bumbling idiot who didn't know how to hold down a conversation without gravely insulting the very people Theo needed on his side to ensure things went smoothly. It would help if they gave her time to breathe, to find her feet, but that wasn't in the agenda.

Everyone wanted a look at the foreign Consort, the woman Theo and Galen had brought back with them out of exile.

Everyone found her... less than impressive.

She couldn't even blame them for that. She was just a normal woman who'd been swept up in something magical. Now, the magic was wearing a little thin and reality intruded more often than not.

You made your choice. You love these men.

Meg slipped out of Galen's arms and tugged him to his feet. "Come on. Let's take a shower and order some food. You know he won't have eaten."

Galen cast a long look at the door, as if revising his timeline to haul Theo back to the room. "Fifteen minutes."

"Sure." She padded into the next room, her bare feet sinking into the thick carpet. The sitting room was for... well, she wasn't really sure what it was for. They didn't take guests in here, except in a rare emergency. It served more as an extra barrier between them and the rest of the palace than anything else.

The main room, though, was only for them. It housed a massive bed that accommodated all three of them—and would probably fit another three people easily—as well as a desk for private correspondence and a small table where they could take meals as they saw fit. It was double the size of the apartment she'd had back in New York, and that wasn't even getting into the ridiculously luxurious bathroom.

"On second thought, maybe a bath would be a better option." Her feet hurt, her back ached, and her entire body felt as if she'd run a marathon instead of sat through a dozen painfully polite conversations that only served to remind her just how out of her depth she was. Alys had set up private lessons to get her up to date on the gaps in her Thalanian education, but they felt like too little, too late.

Meg started the water. The tub was just as massive as everything else seemed to be in this room—bed, shower, the room itself. She knew from personal experience that all three of them could fit into the thing comfortably, but that wasn't on the agenda tonight. Unfortunately. She tested the water one last time and turned to find Galen watching her.

His dark eyes saw too much. "How you holding up?"

"I'm good." She almost sounded like she meant it. When Galen just stared, she sighed. "This is hard and I'm screwing up, okay? I hate feeling like I don't know what I'm doing, and that is all I've felt since we came here." He opened his mouth, but she held up a hand before he could respond. "It doesn't change how I feel about you—either of you—but I'm struggling."

"Did *you* manage to eat today in between spilling tea on Lady Nibley's lap and doing the dozen other things on that agenda Alys put together for you?"

No point in lying. He'd just know, and then he'd give her one of those severe looks that she was too tired to do anything about. "I managed a finger sandwich at lunch."

"Thought so." He shook his head. "Take a bath, baby. I'll go find Theo and order us some food."

She wasn't sure she'd manage to stay awake long enough to eat once she got into the bath, but that was a problem for later. "Sure. Okay." It was only after the words slipped out that she realized a few months ago, she would have argued just to argue. Galen would have snarled back, and she would have gotten in his face a little, until their mutual contrariness transformed to pure sex. He would be fucking her against the bathroom sink right now.

Meg glanced at the sink in question, a sturdy marble creation that could stand a lot of abuse. Maybe she wasn't *that* tired...

But it was too late.

Galen was gone.

AFTER THE LAST meeting on his agenda, Theo found himself

in his personal gym. It wasn't intentional, but the stress of duking it out with Lord Huxley over putting in a new dam on his territory had clicked Theo into autopilot after he'd finished up. And so here he was, dressed in shorts and doing rep after rep until his thoughts stopped racing in circles through his mind.

He needed to see Galen, to touch Meg, but his head wasn't on straight. He'd forgotten, somehow, in his months of exile, just how fucking exhausting it was running a country. It didn't matter that he had the council and plenty of people to delegate various tasks to. At this point in the game, there were only two people he knew he could trust beyond a shadow of a doubt—his Consorts.

Everyone else was suspect.

He moved from the squat rack to the bench press and threw weight onto the bar. His world narrowed down to the next rep, the straining of his muscles, and the sweat coating his skin. He was Theodore Fitzcharles III, King of Thalania, but that didn't mean he stopped being *Theo*. The balance between the two had slid off-kilter the second they all crossed back onto Thalanian soil, and he didn't know how to fix it.

Before his father died...

Grief rose, a wave he spent far too much time dodging. A year gone and it felt like yesterday. Sometimes, being back in the palace, he even forgot himself. He'd glance at the door, half expecting his father to walk through and offer a suggestions about a particularly tricky problem he was working through.

Except that was impossible.

Theo closed his eyes and inhaled deeply. It had been easier with his mother. At ten, he was allowed emotions without worrying about appearing weak and, more importantly, his father had been there to guide him through the storm. He didn't have a map to move through the stages of grief for his father.

Footsteps sounded, as familiar as his own. "I'm almost done."

Silence for a beat, then two. "I'll spot you while you finish up," Galen said.

Theo opened his eyes to see his best friend, his lover, his Consort, standing over him. He looked as tired and worn out as Theo felt, though where Theo had lost weight, Galen had gained muscle. No telling where he found the time to work out, but the evidence was in the way his T-shirt stretched tight across his shoulders and chest and the clear definition in his legs. He couldn't even appreciate the new changes for fear of what they indicated. *Are we going to war, Galen?*

Some days it certainly felt like it.

He finished up his set slowly, drawing in the burning of his muscles as he strained against the weight of the bench press. In this moment, he was perfectly present. It wouldn't last. It never lasted. But he had right now, and it would have to be able to shore him up for the coming conversation.

Theo wiped his face with his towel and stood. "Okay, I'm done. What's wrong?"

"Would you like a list?"

Fuck, something *was* wrong. Theo glanced at the door to the gym, instinctively looking for the audience they had for most of their waking hours. The door remained closed, which didn't mean no one was listening, but it lessened the likelihood. Even with the cameras blinking in the corners of the room, they were as close to alone as they were likely to get. "Galen, talk to me."

"Not tonight. Not like this." Galen started for the door.

"Meg had a hard day, Theo. We all did." Subtle comment, less subtle bite. If he concentrated, Theo could almost see things unraveling around him. He'd known life wouldn't be simple once he retook the throne, but the freedom of exile had gone to his head and he'd forgotten just how easy it could be to drown in this world.

It sure as hell seemed like all three of them were a few short breaths from doing exactly that.

Drowning.

And he didn't know how to fix it.

This wasn't the time or place to get into it. Darkness had fallen while Theo was preoccupied, and most of the palace staff had gone home. It didn't leave the halls empty—they were never empty—but there were fewer people to bow and murmur greetings as he and Galen stalked toward their private suite. Theo managed to nod in response, but he schooled his expression to discourage actual conversation. In his current mood, he couldn't guarantee what he'd say if someone tried to stop him now.

They slammed into their suite and Theo grabbed Galen's arm before he had a chance to leave the sitting room. "What's going on?"

"No. Fuck that. You don't get to play the concerned partner now." Galen shot a look toward the main rooms and lowered his voice. "You got what you wanted, Theo. You got your cake and you're eating it, too. The first King of Thalania in history to name two Consorts. Congratu-fucking-lations."

Theo rocked back on his heels. This conversation had been a long time in coming, and even knowing it bore down on him with all the subtly of a runaway train, he still wasn't prepared. "You knew—"

"No. I don't need to hear that I went into this with eyes wide open. I know I fucking did." Galen dragged a hand over his face. "Meg has three months before school starts up again. She's fucking miserable, Theo. She puts on a brave face for you, but underneath she's messed up."

And what about you?

Theo didn't voice the words lodged in his throat. He'd learned a long time ago not to ask questions he might not want answers to, and this numbered among them. He didn't point out that he'd given both Galen and Meg a chance to leave six months ago, and he sure as hell didn't point out that they could leave now if they were so inclined. He might be an ass sometimes, but not about this.

Not when they'd already sacrificed so much.

He couldn't fix this. Not yet. Things would calm down once he got the Families in line and brought his siblings around. Camilla was happy to see him, of course. Even with their father's death, his baby sister had been kept from the worst of the political bullshit. At sixteen, she was just starting to dip her toes into the water, and he'd do whatever it took to ensure she remained safe while she figured out her own path.

Their brother was another story altogether. For just under a year, Edward had thought he'd be king. Having that taken away, rightfully or no, created a divide between them that Theo didn't know how to fix. Especially when Edward announced his intentions to attend Oxford for university, and left within weeks of Theo's coronation. There were a handful of nobles who'd jump at the chance to use that separation for their own ambitions, and he needed to fix it before things got worse.

But not tonight.

Tonight, he had to fix *this*.

Theo snagged the back of Galen's neck. His friend resisted for a second, but then he exhaled harshly and let

Theo pull him closer until their foreheads pressed together. *Tell me what you need.* Theo closed his eyes. Galen didn't have to tell him. He knew what Galen needed—what they all needed. "Where is she?"

"Tub."

Good. She'd be nice and relaxed. He tightened his grip on Galen's neck. "The food?"

"An hour."

Good boy. Sex wouldn't solve any of the undercurrents in the long term, but it would help release the tension that had been growing with every passing day. Trapping the two people he loved was never part of the plan, but Theo couldn't shake the feeling that was exactly what he'd done. He released Galen and stepped back. "Strip."

Theo turned and walked deeper into the room without bothering to make sure Galen obeyed, knowing it would piss his friend off, and knowing that anger was exactly what he needed to purge the festering feeling beneath. At least for tonight. Tomorrow, they would talk and further clear the air. Open communication was the only way this would work, and they hadn't spent enough time alone together to get to the heart of things in the last couple weeks.

His fault. He knew that well enough.

He'd fix it. He'd find a way to fix *all* of it.

Theo pulled off his shirt and tossed it over the back of the desk chair. He kicked off his shoes and then walked into the bathroom. Steam fogged the mirrors and Meg had turned off all the lights, leaving only the trio of thick candles lit on the half wall between the tub and the sinks. It gave the room a dark, intimate feeling that he approved of. He stalked to the edge of the tub and took a seat near her head. She had her eyes closed and the water licked at her breasts as if determined to offer him teasing glimpses.

"Thought you weren't working late tonight."

"I wasn't planning on it. Things didn't go well with Lord Huxley, and I didn't want to come back here with that frustration riding so close to the surface. I needed some time to cool off." He smoothed a hand over her hair, tangling his fingers in the dark strands. She looked good. The decadent meals the staff insisted on putting together had filled out her curves, and he couldn't count her ribs the way he'd been able to when they first met. Theo kept stroking her hair and used his free hand to urge her onto her stomach. The new position freed him up to work at the knots of tension lining her shoulders and upper back. Tension that was his fault. "Let me take care of you tonight, princess." Galen walked naked into the bathroom and leaned against the counter, crossing his arms over his chest. Theo met his gaze steadily. "Let me take care of both of you."

2

M eg knew what she should do. She should tell Theo that the best way to take care of her and Galen was to *talk* to them. But with the candle-light playing across Theo's skin and his skillful hands working at the knots in her shoulders, she couldn't work up the energy to fight with him. "I'm not happy with you."

"I know." He dug into a particularly tight knot, working it with his thumb. "What do you need from me tonight, princess?"

She let her eyes close, let him keep working his magic on her body. Six months into their relationship, and Meg knew that Theo would give her anything she asked for. If she wanted him and Galen to dress up like Vikings and roleplay one of her favorite scenes in a romance novel she was read-ing, he'd do it without question. He *had* done it without question last month. Theo might be fucking up on commu-nication and overworked to the point where she barely saw him, but she never doubted for a second that he loved her and wanted her happy.

She slipped beneath the surface of the water. Free of his

touch, clarity didn't suddenly strike her like lightning. If there was an answer, she didn't have it. Meg slowly stood and let herself drink in the way Theo watched her. As if she was some kind of Aphrodite rising out of the ocean instead of standing here in their tub. "I just want you tonight, Theo. None of the bullshit. Just you."

He nodded and grabbed one of the ridiculously large towels they kept stocked in here. "Let me take care of you tonight," he repeated.

Easy enough to read in between the lines of what he wanted. A reprieve in a long line of reprieves. Theo was trying to hold off the inevitable conversation all three of them had to have until he could iron out the mess Thalania had become in his absence. Or maybe the backbiting politics and squabbling seven Families had always been like this. Either way, Theo wanted time to get it handled.

She just wished he'd lean on her and Galen a little bit in the meantime.

Meg stepped out of the tub and let him wrap her in the towel. "Like I'm going to say no."

Theo dried her gently, thoroughly, making quick work of it. He had a face built for candlelight, all sharp angles and a beauty that was damn near painful to witness. The passing time should have inoculated her to the sight of him, but then he would turn just so or look at her with those big blue eyes, and she'd forget to breathe.

"You could."

She blinked. "What?"

"You could say no."

Meg laughed. She couldn't help it. "Theo, have you looked in the mirror lately?"

He glanced over, and she followed his gaze to the large mirror situated on the other side of the bath. They painted quite the picture, him large and towering over her, his shock of near-black hair several shades darker than hers, his big hands holding the towel against her skin. For once, he wasn't wearing his usual clothing of suits that cost enough to give Meg hives. In the workout shorts, he looked... Not normal. Theo would never be anything as mundane as normal.

He looked touchable.

So that was exactly what she did. Meg ran her hands up his stomach to his chest and stepped to him. "I know I could say no. I've said no to you more times than I can count since we've met." She cupped his strong jaw with her palm. "Theo, are you okay?"

"No." He pulled her slowly, inexorably closer, until her breasts pressed against his bare chest. "Just... Let me take care of you tonight, princess."

The rare vulnerability he let her see in that moment seduced her as thoroughly as his body ever had. She nodded. "Yes."

Theo swept her off her feet and carried her out of the bathroom. Normally, she'd give him shit for such a caveman move, but Meg didn't want to poke at him tonight. She was tired and heartsore, and both her men were obviously feeling the same. They couldn't fix the mess waiting for them outside those doors, but they could strengthen their foundations tonight.

She just hoped it would be enough.

Galen waited for them on the bed, clothed in only his skin. Her heart skipped a beat. As much as Theo's beauty seduced her, Galen's raw sex appeal knocked her right in the stomach. His dusky skin was crisscrossed with lighter scars, a testament to the abuse his father had leveled at him as a child. His dark hair had grown longer, losing the military-like cut. She liked it. There was a lot to like about Galen.

He watched Theo carry her toward him with a predatory look that sent a bolt of desire through her. Only good things came from Galen getting *that* expression on his face.

Theo set her on the bed just out of reach and pressed a hand to her shoulder. "Don't move." He was only gone a moment, disappearing back into the bathroom and reappearing with a hairbrush. He took up a position against the headboard and urged her to sit between his legs with her back to him.

Theo began carefully combing her wet hair.

Meg closed her eyes and let the gentle tug of the brush soothe her. The fluffy towel and Theo's proximity kept her cozy, but Galen's attention pricked along her skin, a promise of things to come. On and on it went. Theo was never one to do things halfway, but he seemed to enjoy the slow slide of the brush through her drying hair as much as she did.

Finally, he set the brush aside and eased her back against his chest. Her hair was almost dry at this point, but Theo moved its soft weight off her neck and pressed a kiss to her throat. He pulled the towel away from her body and tossed it off the bed, leaving them skin to skin. It felt good to be wrapped up in him like this. Even better than his combing her hair.

The mattress dipped and Meg opened her eyes to find Galen had moved to a point just past their feet for a better view. He arched a dark eyebrow at her, but something soft and intimate marred the arrogance of the expression. He needed this reaffirming as much as she did.

For once, no one colored the air around them with filthy words and dirty talk. Theo stroked his hands over her body, the rough slide of his palms across her skin sending her nerves sparking in response. She writhed a little, but he wouldn't be guided. He paid equal attention to her arms, her shoulders, her stomach and her hips, avoiding her breasts and pussy.

The damn tease.

Finally, a small eternity later, he cupped her breasts, giving them the same slow exploration delivered to the rest of her body. Meg couldn't stop herself from arching up to press herself more firmly into his hands.

"Impatient," he murmured against her skin.

"Can you blame her?" Galen's rough tone made Meg shiver. He reached down and palmed his own cock. "She's shaking with need."

Meg grabbed Theo's hand. She spread her legs wide, hooking them on either side of Theo's, making sure to give Galen a good show. "Take care of me, baby." She pressed his hand to her pussy. "You promised."

"I did, didn't I?" Theo cupped her there roughly, possessively, the touch lighting a spark beneath Meg's skin. He pushed a single finger into her, still teasing, not offering nearly enough of what she craved. His voice curled around her, just as intimate as their current position. "I'm feeling generous tonight, princess, so I'll let you choose how we give it to you. Do you want me here?" He pushed a second finger into her and then withdrew. "Or here." Theo pressed his wet fingers to her ass.

Meg shivered. "Galen takes the other?"

"You wouldn't deny him, would you?"

As if she didn't spend far too much of her time craving the feeling of being pinned between them in every way possible, both their cocks filling her until she lost herself completely. Of the unique closeness and trust that came from this particular kind of fucking.

"In fact..." Theo slid his hands beneath her ass and lifted her higher against his chest. "Come have a taste, Galen. An appetizer for both of you."

Galen didn't hesitate. He crawled up the mattress to lay between their spread thighs and adjusted Meg against Theo's body until he had her where he wanted her. Unlike Theo, Galen didn't tease this time. He just descended on her pussy like he could work out all his frustration with his tongue on her clit.

Theo kept her pinned in place with one hand on her hip, but the other he laced through Galen's hair, holding his face against her. As if he wasn't already fucking her with his tongue like he could never get enough.

Pleasure coiled inside her, tighter and tighter. She reached down and covered Theo's hand with hers and used her other to lace through Galen's hair on the other side of his head. "Oh god, Galen. That feels so good."

He growled against her skin, the sound vibrating her clit. Theo laughed softly. "Can you feel how she tenses when you do that? She's so fucking close."

His words and Galen's mouth were too much. Galen sucked her clit hard and that was it. Meg orgasmed, writhing against him even as he softened his touch to the barest brushing of his breath against her sensitized skin.

"Mmm." Galen gave her one last lick and rose over their bodies to give first Theo and then Meg a devastating kiss. "Now we're getting somewhere."

Meg turned in Theo's arms and climbed up to straddle him, well aware that he allowed her to do it. She hesitated, but he didn't give her a chance to decide how to play this. He guided her down onto his cock, slowly and surely spearing her to the hilt, his hands on her hips locking her in place. She felt more than heard Galen move away to grab the lube they kept stocked in the nightstand and return to take up a place behind her.

She tensed. She couldn't help it.

No matter how many times they did this, how intensely she craved the whole experience, there was always a moment of *oh god, I've made a mistake* as the second cock pushed into her. This time offered no exception.

Galen ran his hand up her spine even as he sank another inch into her ass, slowly and steadily working deeper. "Breathe, baby."

"We've got you." Theo cradled her face and kissed her softly, his lips and tongue devastatingly gentle, the feeling all the more overwhelming because of the almost-uncomfortable way they filled her. The stroke of his tongue against hers told her more clearly than words how much he cherished her, how much he loved her.

And then Galen was sheathed in her completely and he pressed his big body against her back, caging her and setting her free at the same time. Meg closed her eyes and allowed the feeling to wash over her as she relaxed into the feeling of them inside her. If she concentrated, she could almost feel their heartbeats on either side of her body, a merging of them into something more.

Theo smoothed her hair back. "Good?" His normally smooth voice had roughened, the only signal of his need to move.

"Yes." The word broke in the middle. She cleared her throat. "I'm good."

Galen lifted himself off her enough so she could move, a slow drag of her body between theirs. His weight pressed her clit hard against Theo's pubic bone, and every slide had her relaxing a little more, welcoming the penetration and the orgasm sparking to life inside her. Each stroke built on that pleasure, and Meg fought to keep her rhythm consistent. She bit her bottom lip, trapping a whimper threatening to break free. It was too much. Between one breath and the next, she came. Her men held her through the waves that seemed to go on and on. It might have been seconds or hours, but finally it released her and she slumped against Theo's chest.

They shifted her onto her side and came with her. Galen kissed the back of her neck and reached around to cup her breasts, playing with her nipples. Theo hitched her leg up and out, opening her completely to them. He took her mouth as he and Galen began to move, chasing their own pleasure.

Careful, though. They were so damn careful with her.

Galen lost himself first, pulling out of her in time to come in harsh spurts against her back. Theo drove into her, grinding hard as he came, still kissing her in that devastatingly gentle way.

They lay there for several long moments, but before reality—and their level of stickiness—could sink in, Theo rose and carried her into the shower. Galen joined them several minutes later and they washed each other leisurely.

She loved this just as much as the fucking. The casual intimacy of Galen handing Theo the shampoo, of him rolling his eyes as she washed his back, of the soft kisses they both pressed to her skin in passing as they went through the motions of cleaning themselves and each other.

The bed had clean sheets on it—the reason for Galen's delay—when they made it back into the bedroom. Meg glanced at Theo, a thousand questions lingering in her chest, but ultimately exhaustion weighed too heavily.

Tomorrow. Tomorrow. They would have a conversation tomorrow.

Tomorrow just hadn't come around once in six months.

Galen dropped onto his side of the bed and, for all intents and purposes, appeared to pass out immediately. She laughed softly and pulled the comforter higher around her shoulders. Laying between them was like occupying space between two space heaters. She loved it, couldn't get enough of it. Meg rolled over to find Theo scrolling through his phone. "Can't the emails wait until tomorrow?"

"Just a few small things to take care of."

There were an endless supply of *just a few small things*, but she didn't say as much. Theo reached over and absently ran his hand along her back. Up and down, tracing abstract patterns over her skin.

Meg tried to stay awake. She really did. But his touch was like a drug. In the end, she didn't stand a chance. Weights attached themselves to her eyelids and she relaxed into the absurdly soft mattress and pillow, safe and secure between the two men she loved.

3

Theo was gone when Galen woke up. He'd known it would happen from the moment his friend ordered him to strip last night. The fucking phenomenal sex didn't make up for the fact that things weren't working in their current situation. Theo wasn't normally the kind of man to dodge hard conversations and impossible scenarios, but none of them had fully anticipated what being in Thalania would do to them, individually and as a unit.

Nothing was the same.

"Morning."

He turned to find Meg watching him. She was tucked under a mound of blankets so that only her face was free, her dark hair a tangled wave over her pillow. She got cold when she slept, and the only time that seemed to abate was when she was sandwiched between him and Theo. The amount of blankets around her gave him a pretty solid timeline about when Theo left their bed. Early.

The old, familiar anger wrapped around him. When

they were younger, he could channel it into productive things, but there was nothing more useless than being a fucking Consort. Galen didn't do the political bullshit. He didn't pretty up his words, and he didn't bother to play nice to people who would just as happily stab him with a steak knife as pass the salt over dinner. The problem remained that being the Consort required exactly that skillset.

Meg frowned. "What's going on in that head of yours?"

He didn't want to say it. They'd made promises when they decided to stay, and bitching about the consequences was worthless. He refused to give up Theo or Meg, which meant he was stuck as playing Consort for... Fuck, forever.

If that wasn't depressing, Galen didn't know what was. He couldn't tell her, though. "Have you thought about school?"

Instantly, her expression closed down. Meg sat up. "What kind of question is that?"

"A legit one. Theo said you had options when you decided to stay. It's been six months. You'll have to make a decision at some point."

She rolled her eyes. "Thank you, Galen. I wouldn't have possibly known how long it's been without you reminding me."

All too tempting to poke and prod her into a fight. Meg was good for it. She and Galen were too similar for anyone's peace of mind, and he knew exactly what buttons to push to provoke a response. They'd fight and then they'd fuck, and then they'd go about their respective days with nothing having changed.

But Meg surprised him. One second she was glaring like she wanted to smother him with one of her pillows and the next she was straddling his stomach. She planted her hands on his chest and gave him a long look. "What's really bothering you?"

Galen played through it in his mind. He'd sit up, toppling her to the mattress, and then his mouth would be on her pussy and she wouldn't be worried about anything but her next orgasm. There would be no thought or energy left for uncomfortable questions.

She must have seen something on his face because she frowned and poked his chest. "Communication, Galen. You promised me honesty and communication."

Damn it. There was no getting around this.

Maybe he didn't *want* to get around it. He'd meant what he said to Theo last night—time was ticking and Meg wasn't exactly exuding a happy vibe lately. Theo couldn't leave Thalania, not with the crown on his head and the throne under his ass. There were no term limits on the monarchy. Galen wouldn't leave Theo. This life might not look anything like he'd pictured it, but Theo had no one to watch his back in this nest of harpies. Galen couldn't leave him. Not to mention the fact he loved the bastard.

The only thing leashing Meg to them was love, and love didn't always last.

Something akin to panic seized his chest. It wasn't supposed to be like this. A year ago, he had a solid plan; get Theo back on the throne and take down his treacherous uncle in the process. Keep Theo safe in the process. That was it.

Now they had Meg, and Galen had his hands tied with this Consort shit, and he couldn't protect the only two people in this fucked up world he actually loved.

Knock that shit off. You don't deal in daydreams and wishes. Name the reality. Adapt as necessary. He ran his hands up

Meg's legs to bracket her thighs. Communication. It wouldn't solve this particular problem, but he'd be damned before he did something to alienate her further. "Show me yours, I'll show you mine."

"Pretty sure that line hasn't worked at any point in history." She idly traced the most ragged scar that ran across his upper chest. "Okay, fine. I'll play. Yes, I've thought about school. I only have a year left, and as much as I've learned that plans have to be allowed to change, I don't want *this* to change." She hesitated, obviously weighing whether to go on. "This, all of this, isn't really mine. I know I'm Consort, but I'm only in the position because Theo put me there. I also know that even if things went horribly wrong between all of us he would never just... turn me out on the street. But, right now, my entire life is dependent on him and I can't stop playing doomsday scenarios in my head. I want my degree. I want my *career*. I just don't know how I'm supposed to take classes when Alys has me scheduled down to my bathroom breaks."

Galen kept stroking her thighs, the touch calming a part of him he didn't know how to put into words. "You could scale back your responsibilities."

"If I do that, it means *you* end up with more on your plate." She gave a sharp shake of her head. "We agreed on the plan that first couple weeks—divide and conquer. Theo needs the Families' support, and the best way to do that is through us paving the way." Meg made a face. "I just didn't expect to screw up so frequently. There's an art to this political crap, and I don't have it."

He cupped her hips, letting his thumbs play over her skin. This casual intimacy was something Galen never got enough of. Theo used to be the only person he'd shared it with. Galen didn't let anyone else close enough to try. Intimacy required trust, and he'd seen time and time again how effectively trust could be twisted to hurt and manipulate. It was something his old man had always been particularly skilled at.

His old man. Dorian Mikos. One of the people that helped orchestrate Theo losing his throne in the first place. The bastard had slipped away right around the time Galen and the others were crossing Thalania's border.

Out of Thalania, out of their jurisdiction, out of the justice he deserved.

Galen didn't doubt for a second that they hadn't seen the last of his father, but everyone's energy had become devoted to the more present issues that kept showing up. He considered Meg's words. "It's not failing to have to reconfigure."

"Really? Because no one else has had to *reconfigure*. I'm the weak link."

"No." He sat up and framed her face with his hands. "You're better than that self-pitying shit. You know damn well that I'm struggling, too. Fuck, *Theo* is struggling, though he's too proud to admit it. This hasn't been easy on any of us."

Meg stared him down. "How would I know that, Galen? We barely talk anymore. We scurry and rush around and fuck until we can't see straight, and then rinse and repeat the next day."

This was worse than he'd realized.

Liar. You knew exactly how bad it had gotten. You just didn't want to face it.

Theo would know what to say to calm Meg's fears. Theo, that asshole, always knew what to say. It wasn't a gift Galen possessed. He didn't have gentle words or reassurances. He just had the stark truth. "Being back here feels like being in my childhood home again."

Meg froze as if she'd just stumbled into a clearing and noticed a wolf slinking through the trees. She opened her mouth, seemed to reconsider, and finally said, "Oh?"

Fuck, this was his fault, too. Galen didn't talk about his childhood. Theo knew all the details—he'd been there for the aftermath and the nightmares and all the bullshit Galen went through before he pulled himself together—but he hadn't talked about it with Meg other than in broad strokes. Not about the scars. Not about his father. Not about how fucked his reality had been.

He didn't want to talk about it now, either.

Too late. He laced his fingers through her hair, smoothing it back from her face. They were too close, too intimate, her big hazel eyes threatening to expose his shredded soul, but if he set her back now, she'd see it as a rejection. "Ever since I moved into the palace when I was sixteen, I had a role set out for me. Theo needed someone to watch his back, someone he could trust, and I was that someone. I always intended to be his head of security, and even when we were fighting to get him out of exile, that was the plan. As head of security, no one expected me to play politics or mince words." He was just himself, an identity completely divorced of his parents' treasonous history.

"Now you don't have that option."

"Now I don't have that option," he agreed. "It's like wearing a too-tight jacket. I can't breathe. And every time I think about how happy my douchebag of a father must be to have a Mikos named as Consort, it fucks up my head. This is not who I am."

"The things we do for love, huh?" Meg gave a sad smile.

"This happily ever after is more complicated than I would have guessed."

Galen pressed a soft kiss to her forehead. "Things will even out. The Families all retreat back to their respective estates over the summer, so that will be a welcome relief." A Band-Aid. It was all he had to offer in the way of comfort, and it was nowhere near good enough. "We will figure it out, baby. Just hang in there for a little while longer."

"I'm not tapping out. That's not what this is about. I'm just... I'm so tired, Galen. And there's no end in sight."

"I know." He glanced at the clock and cursed. "We better get ready."

"Yeah." She didn't sound any more excited about it than he felt, but Meg climbed off him and padded to the bathroom.

Galen dropped back to the mattress and stared at the ceiling. They were going to lose her. It had always been a possibility, but with shit going the way it was, the possibility was rapidly sliding from theoretical into a sure thing.

And he didn't know what to do to stop it.

BY THE TIME Meg headed to her tea date with Noemi, her mood had gone from grumpy straight into foul. She kept replaying the last twelve hours in her head—Theo's promise to take care of them, the admittedly outstanding sex, talking with Galen that morning. Galen was better at hiding his emotions than she was, but he was *hurting*. And she couldn't fix it. She wasn't even sure *Theo* could fix it, but he'd damn well better try.

A familiar figure hovered in the doorway ahead and Meg gave her first genuine smile in hours. "Cami."

Theo's little sister jumped like she'd been caught doing something wrong. She was a cute little thing, and at sixteen, she still had a little bit of childhood in her face. She wore jeans and a flowing shirt, and her dark hair was pulled back into a no-nonsense ponytail. "Oh, uh, hi, Meg."

Yeah, she was definitely doing something she wasn't supposed to be. Meg glanced around, but aside from her and Alys, no one was in evidence. "Looking for someone?"

Cami glanced at Alys, clearly not interested in sharing anything with her close. Meg didn't even hesitate. She turned to the other woman and gave a small smile. "Could we have some privacy, please?"

Alys clutched her ever-present tablet. "We're under a tight schedule, Consort."

Irritation flared. She knew they were under a tight schedule. Alys liked to remind her every time she stopped the forward dash from meeting to meal to tea to meeting. There were only seven Families in Thalania, but the heads of each had dozens and dozens of children and grandchildren and, in some cases, great-grandchildren. And Meg was expected to entertain the half that qualified as feminine persuasion.

But none of that was Alys's fault, so she fought to keep her tone light. "I think Noemi will be fine for a few more minutes." She injected enough steel into her words that Alys got the picture. This was non-negotiable.

Alys finally nodded. "Five minutes."

I'll take as long as I damn well please. Meg didn't stay it, couldn't say it. "Thank you." She took Cami's arm and led her a bit down the hallway to a door that led into one of the many unused sitting rooms. Some ancestor of Theo's, in peak Rich People Mentality, decided that he didn't want to entertain in the same space, so he had fifty-two sitting rooms peppered throughout the palace so he could use a different one for each week of the year. They'd been slowly redone by the various queens who'd come and gone since then, and these days they were great places to grab a quiet conversation, though Meg had stumbled in on at least two couples making other use of the spaces.

She really hoped she wasn't about to stumble onto a third with her boyfriend's underage sister in tow.

Thankfully, the room was empty. It housed three delicate chairs and an equally delicate couch, all made of a pale spiraling design and floral cushions. "This should do nicely." She shut the door and took a seat on the nearest chair, giving Cami time to make what she would of the situation.

When she'd come here, she'd expected Theo's siblings to be spoiled assholes. Meg really should have known better. Edward had been kind of a little prick before he left for Oxford, but that was as much from having been raised under Theo's shadow as his age—eighteen. Cami was... not fragile, exactly, though everyone treated her like she was made of spun glass. She was perfectly polite to Meg, but she resisted any overtures of friendship.

Cami perched on the edge of one of the chairs. She smoothed her shirt down and sighed. "This will sound silly."

"Try me."

"Lady Nibley is in the palace today, and she's supposed to be meeting with my brother this afternoon."

Okay, that was the last thing Meg expected to hear. "Yes, I had tea with her yesterday." The old woman with her freaking pimp cane had played an instrumental part in Theo regaining his throne, and even though she didn't seem to know what to think of Meg, she was a refreshing breath of fresh air every time they interacted. It didn't happen often enough—Lady Nibley preferred to spend her time in her estate near the Mediterranean Sea in the southern portion of Thalania. "I thought she was heading home today."

"She is." Cami's fingers fluttered against her jeans. "But she came here because she wants Theo to convince her grandson to come home, and she's dragging her feet about leaving before he promises to see it done."

This was all news. "Okay."

"There was an incident when her grandson was a child. He went missing for a very long time, and only recently has it come out that he's alive and well."

Meg waited, sure the girl would get to her point eventually. This was all interesting, but she missed the part where Cami had a reason to care. "I'm glad he's okay."

"I don't know if *okay* is a good word for it." Cami fiddled with the hem of her shirt, all confined nervous movement. "He won't come back to Thalania, and our father couldn't convince him to change his mind. Lady Nibley thinks Theo can succeed where our father failed."

She didn't check the clock ticking on the table next to the door, but Meg could practically feel Alys's impatience on the other side. "Cami," she said gently. "While I'm sure that's very tragic for the Nibley family, I'm a little confused on why it's got you lurking in the hallways."

"We're promised."

Meg blinked. "What?"

"When we were children, our parents had an arrangement in which I was promised to him." Cami stared hard at the floral pattern on the rug beneath their feet. "He went missing almost immediately after, but he's been found and I'm sure Lady Nibley will want to see it brought to fruition."

She was still trying to catch up. "But... Does Theo know?

I can't imagine he'd authorize his little sister playing the part of a child bride."

"It's nothing like that." Cami made a face. "I get a choice, of course. My father always stressed that part. It's just..." She hesitated and, for a moment, Meg was sure she'd wilt. She underestimated the princess. Cami jerked her chin up and her shoulders back, meeting her gaze directly. "No one ever tells me anything. If my brother is organizing a retrieval of my so-called betrothed, I should be involved. I know I'm only sixteen, but at my age, Theo was already running some of our father's operations within the country. Edward was in training in addition to his schooling. I'm just... here."

Ah. Feeling useless wasn't something Meg had ever dealt with—at least not as a teenager. She'd been too focused on getting out of the hellhole she grew up in to worry about her place in life. All she'd cared about was that it wasn't *there*, in that trailer, following in the footsteps of the mother who seemed intent on drinking herself to death and bringing everyone in her life down alongside her. There hadn't been time for doubt. There was only Meg's plan. "What do you want to do?"

"I don't know." She finally dropped her gaze. "I don't even know what my options are. I don't want to marry some guy who I haven't seen since I was four." She lowered her voice. "And he was so *old*."

From what Meg understood, Cami should have had more freedom than either of her brothers when it came to who she married. Her children would likely never end up on the throne, so it *should* have allotted her a wider choice in partners. "How about this?" Meg pushed to her feet. "Why don't you meet me after I have tea with Noemi, and we'll sit down and figure something out? If you want to be treated like an adult, then going to Theo directly instead of sneaking around is your best bet." Cami would have to find a way to pin him in place long enough to have that conversation, but Meg would help. It was the least she could do that this point—and it had the bonus of being something she actually *wanted* to do.

"You'd do that?"

"Of course." She took the girl's hand and gave it what she hoped was a comforting squeeze. "Now, come on. I think Alys might have a stroke if I'm late for this tea."

"You're probably right." Cami made a face. "Tea with Noemi, huh?"

There was such a teenager tone of disgust in her voice that Meg burst out laughing. "I take it you're not a fan?"

"Oh, it's not that exactly. She's nice enough—nicer than a lot of the other nobles. She's just..." Cami made a vague gesture. "Perfect. Every time I'm in the same room as her, I feel like I'm looking in one of those backlit makeup mirrors that display your every pore and imperfection. I feel dull."

Meg cast a critical look over the girl. Cami was anything but *dull*. She had inherited her father's bone structure—same as Theo had—and if she stopped doing her best to blend into the background, she would own any room she walked into. Part of that would come with age and confidence, but maybe Meg could help her out on that note, too. She was hardly a fashionista, but she was old enough to know a few tricks. That said... "Do you *want* the kind of attention Noemi gets?"

Cami hesitated. "No, not really. Maybe at some point but... No. I already feel like I live under a microscope as it is and the last thing I want right now is more of that."

The teen years. Meg could still vividly remember the push and pull of wanting to fit in with everyone else and wanting to stand out in a way that made other girls in her grade shine. She'd never discovered the knack for it, but then, very few people did. "Come on." She pulled Cami to her feet and led the way to the door.

Alys met them there, her blue eyes wide. "Cami, the King is looking for you." She shot a panicked glance at Meg. "Can you find your way to the tea room down on the main floor? Just follow this hallway to the stairs, down them, two lefts, one right, and it's the third door on the right."

Meg did her best to memorize the harried instructions. "I've got it." She gave Cami's hand another squeeze. "Come find me later if you need me."

"I will. And Meg? Thanks." Cami hurried off with Alys, leaving Meg staring after them. She didn't let herself think about the conversation too long. Palace life was complicated enough without her showing up late for tea. Noemi had never done anything truly terrible—or even been rude— but that feeling of being three inches tall was a sensation Meg shared with Cami. Even though she knew better, she couldn't help comparing herself to the other woman.

Damn it, she knew better than to indulge in that kind of thinking.

They *weren't* in competition with each other across any platform, and disliking Noemi just because she was beautiful and poised and perfect was a bitchy thing to do. Meg's best friend from New York would reach across the damn ocean to slap some sense into her if she knew how Meg was letting this whole thing get to her.

She started down the hallway, picking up her pace. No, she couldn't do a damn thing about being late today, but she would stop dodging the other woman. Noemi may never be a friend, but Meg wouldn't know one way or another unless she gave the woman a chance. Today, she'd do exactly that. She reached the top of the stairs, but a rustling sound behind her stopped her in her tracks. The small hairs on the back of Meg's neck raised and she started to turn to see who was behind her.

She never got the chance.

Hands planted themselves on her upper back and shoved. Meg screamed and scrambled for the bannister, but it was too late. She tipped over the edge and down the stairs.

4

Theo rushed through the palace, ignoring people who called his name or tried to get his attention. Four words repeated in his head, delivered by his pale and shaking sister. *There's been an accident.* An accident involving Meg. A fall. A doctor was already with her.

And he'd just *now* been told.

He knew he should slow down, knew that sprinting down the hallways wasn't something a king was supposed to do, but his rational brain took a backseat to the need to see her. To make sure she was okay. *No, not okay. If she was okay, she wouldn't have had* an accident. He reached the private wing and burst through the door, barely pausing to shut it behind him before he ran into the bedroom.

Meg lay on the bed and she held up a hand the second she saw him. "It's not as bad as it looks."

Doctor Oakes didn't glance up from the bandage he was applying to her arm. "She had the fortune of getting her arm through the bannister before she fell too far. It dislocated her shoulder, which I've corrected. It will be sore, and depending on how she's feeling in the morning, she should wear a sling at least until jarring it doesn't cause any level of discomfort. The rest are just bruises that look alarming, but have caused no lasting damage."

Meg didn't look *alarming*. She looked like she'd been dragged behind a fucking car.

A bruise spread across one side of her face and it was already darkening to a truly terrifying shade of purple. Theo traced its path with his gaze, his stomach lurching when he realized how close she'd come to hitting her temple. Her cheekbone had taken the worst of the damage, but a few inches to the side and they might not be having this conversation right now. "What happened?"

She met his eyes and lied to his face. "I fell."

Goddamn it, princess, what the fuck are you thinking? Theo turned away, shoving his rage into a spot deep inside. Now wasn't the time or place for an emotional response, no matter how furious he was over her lying about something this important. He looked around the room, only now registering that Galen wasn't present. "Where is he?"

"Not in the palace."

Theo sent her a sharp look. Surely... The thought didn't bother to complete itself. Galen would sooner throw himself out a window than lay a hand on Meg. Theo pulled out his phone and, after the slightest hesitation, walked into the bathroom and shut the door behind him. He trusted Meg, and he trusted the doctor to take care of Meg, but she was lying to him and he didn't know why. Better to have this conversation privately.

Galen picked up on the second ring. "What happened?"

Something small and painful lodged in Theo's chest. Of course Galen would know that his calling in the middle of the day meant an emergency and wasn't simply because Theo wanted to talk to him. *Where did this go so wrong?* He set the question aside, just like he'd been setting personal things aside for the last six months. Theo stopped being just a person the second the crown rested on his head. He was the King of Thalania, and as Galen used to be so fond of telling him, his happiness didn't mean shit in the grand scheme of things.

"Theo?"

"Meg's hurt." Two little words to encompass the fear that still clamped around his chest, a vise he didn't know how to loosen. "There was no lasting damage, but she dislocated her shoulder and she looks like shit." He glanced at the door. "She says she fell, but—"

"But that's bullshit. Did anyone see anything?"

"I don't know. I didn't have time to conduct a full investigation as I was sprinting through the halls." He hadn't even thought to check the cameras to see what they'd caught.

The background noise on the line increased, as if Galen had stepped out of a building or car. "I'll take care of it. Stay with her until I get back. Once we know what happened, we'll figure out the next steps."

As if he'd leave Meg in her current condition. *Galen doesn't know that, not anymore.* The feeling in his chest got worse. "I'm not going anywhere."

"Good." Galen hung up.

Once upon a time, Galen never would have thought to question Theo staying by Meg's side until they knew for sure what had happened—and that the threat had passed. Something else to be dealt with later. The number of things they never quite got around to talking about only grew over time. If they weren't careful, it would crush them.

Theo took a moment to splash some water onto his face and, when he finally walked back into the bedroom, he had his kingly mask back in place. The doctor was packing up his things. "There is a bottle of pain medication on the nightstand. Maybe you can talk some sense into her." He gave a short bow and left the room.

"His bedside manner is almost as crappy as Galen's." Meg leaned against a small mountain of pillows, watching him. When they first met, every thought flickered across her features, there for the reading. Somewhere along the way, his princess had learned to lie. Or maybe she'd always known and never bothered with the skill until recently. Impossible to say.

He picked up the orange bottle of little white pills and considered them. "You'll have one before you go to sleep."

"Theo." She shook her head and winced. "I'm not taking anything more than ibuprofen, and you damn well know it."

"They won't make you sick if you're unconscious." He set the bottle back down and climbed onto the mattress to sit next to her. For the first time in as long as they'd known each other, he didn't know how to move forward. She *lied* to him, and not about something mundane or meaningless. But then, Meg always knew where to best play her cards, even when she was in over her head. "Let me hold you, princess?"

She twisted carefully to face him. "Are you asking me or telling me?"

Fuck, he didn't know how to do this. Theo didn't *do* unsure. He came into this world knowing his place and even when that place was temporarily lost to him, he never doubted for an instant that it was *his*. Even with Galen, he'd always taken for granted that they would find a way forward, a way to be together. When he met Meg, she became included in that assumption. They fit, and so they would figure it out.

He couldn't assume anything anymore.

"I'm asking."

Meg scooted closer, and he carefully put his arm around her and waited while she arranged herself against his side. She sighed. "This is a mess."

"How are you feeling?" Careful, tentative question.

She shifted closer. "I feel like shit. My face is one big throbbing pain and my shoulder chimes in with every breath to let me know how pissed off it is."

He sifted his fingers through her hair, ensuring he stayed well away from her bruised cheekbone. "It could have been a lot worse. Those stairs killed my great-great-aunt."

"Of course they did." She huffed out a sound that might have been a laugh under different circumstances. "Is there any part of this palace that isn't haunted by the actions and deaths of your family?"

He wished he had a different answer to the question. "No. Thalania likes its history, even the ugly parts." *Especially* the ugly parts, in some cases.

"How are we doing, Theo? And before you give me some pat answer, I mean how are we really doing? It's been six months. Are you making any progress?"

He wanted to give her a pat response, to soothe away the worry evident in her tone. But Theo couldn't demand honesty—something he fully intended on doing—if he wasn't willing to give her honesty in return. "It's slow. Really slow. Three of the Families have decided that they're not interested in actively working with me, though they haven't gone so far as to work *against* my policies yet. Huxley is out. Lady Nibley is in, with the condition of a favor."

"Her grandson."

He smiled against her hair. "So you heard about that."

"How does she expect you to do something no one in her family has been able to?"

"I'm the King." Such a simple answer, and yet so fucking complex. He'd been trained to ride these ebbs and flows of politics since he was a child, but Theo never remembered it being so exhausting. *My father was alive before. I hadn't realized how much his presence shielded me until it was gone. Until he was gone.*

"Being King doesn't mean you're a god." She draped her arm over his stomach and exhaled. "God, this hurts."

"I know, princess." He pressed a soft kiss to her unmarked temple. "Do you want to tell me the truth about what happened or should we wait for Galen to view the video and let him yell at you once he gets back to the room?"

She tensed. "I don't know what you're talking about."

"Yes, you do."

"I fell—"

He spoke right over her, his earlier fear surging up and pouring out of his mouth in the form of anger. "What I don't understand is why you're bothering to lie at all. You didn't fall down those stairs, Meg, so don't treat me like a fucking idiot by saying you did."

"Maybe I didn't want you to react like this and start storming through the palace looking for the responsible party. If I knew who'd done it, I would have told you, but it's just some nameless person and I can't have you on a rampage when you're already walking a fine enough line as it is."

Fuck him.

She wasn't lying for whatever the hell he'd thought her misguided reasoning was. She was lying to protect *him.*

Theo sagged back against the headboard and stared at the ceiling. "You have to be able to talk to me, Meg. You have to trust that I'm not going to react like... I don't even know what the fuck to call that. You have to know I can handle it."

"I know you can handle it. That's not what I'm saying." She kept her head tucked against his chest, making it impossible to look into her eyes. "You just shouldn't have to."

"This isn't some petty bullshit. You could have died." Saying the words slammed him back into the car crash seven months ago that was no more an accident than her fall had been. To seeing Meg, pale and unconscious, too much of her blood covering the ground around her.

It could happen again.

It almost had.

Theo had to concentrate to keep his hold on her light and not clutch her to him as if he could keep her safe from whoever meant her harm. He'd already proven abysmal at it. She was in this situation *because* of him. "Do you want to leave?"

Meg shot up, nearly clipping his chin with the top of her head. "Don't you dare."

"Don't I dare, what?"

She sat back and raised a shaking finger to wave it in his face. "Don't you dare try to send me away. We went over this last time. I'm not going anywhere, and damn you to hell for even thinking of suggesting it." She glared, the effect only stronger by the impressive bruise coloring the side of her face. "Do you love me, Theo?"

If he was smart, he'd lie to her. Tell her that yes, he cared about her, but it was best if she went back to New York, back to her safe life and her equally safe plan for the future. The worst she had to deal with back there was drunk bar patrons, and Meg had already proved herself more than capable. She wouldn't be in active danger in New York.

But Theo had promised her honesty. "Yes, I love you."

"Then let's not play the guilt game. This isn't your fault,

and trying to send me away is just going to result in a fight that you won't win."

"Meg—"

The door opened and heavy footsteps signaled Galen's arrival. The fact that they heard him at all was a testament to how worried he was. Normally, he was more ghost than man.

Galen stopped in the doorway, visibly centering himself. "She was pushed." He gave Meg a long look that communicated just how pissed he was that she'd bothered to try to lie about it, and then turned his attention to Theo. "Whoever it was knew where the cameras were. They wore a black sweatshirt and pants. I can't even narrow down gender—a woman or a small man."

The palace alone staffed well over a hundred people, all of who moved through the space regularly and would know where the cameras were. Add in the nobles and their various staff and that number more than doubled. It could be anyone.

Meg gave a soft laugh. "Your aunt did warn me that people here would want to kill me."

"That's not funny."

"Never said it was."

They looked at each other, the truth an almost physical presence in the room with them. Someone had tried to kill Meg. They failed, but there was no reason to think that would deter them.

Galen crossed his arms over his chest. "I'm going to talk to Isaac. We're putting security on you."

"You *have* security on me."

"Only when you're outside the palace. Now, they're on you all the time."

Meg thinned her lips like she wanted to argue, but whatever she saw on their faces changed her mind. "Fine."

Galen stalked closer to the bed. "Did they give her something?"

Meg started to cross her arms over her chest, winced, and let herself sink back into the pillows. "For the millionth time, I am sitting *right here* and talking about me like I'm a woman-shaped doll doesn't fly. No, the doctor didn't give me anything."

Theo grabbed the pain meds and gave them a shake. "On the contrary."

"Shut up, you tattletale," she hissed.

Galen kicked off his shoes. "Look, baby, I know the pain pills make you nauseous, but what's the alternative?" He climbed onto the bed to sit on the other side of her and lifted her hair away from her face. "Fuck. You look like shit."

"Thanks, *baby*. You really know how to turn a girl's head with that kind of talk."

The acidity in her tone rolled off Galen just like it always seemed to. They bickered as often as they fucked, and it bonded them in a way that had nothing to do with Theo. Normally, evidence of that love made him happy, but today it felt like he was standing on the outside of a window and looking in.

Galen shifted to cup Meg's jaw and tilted her head to the side. "We'll order some soup—something you don't have to chew—and crackers. If you put something substantial in your stomach before you take the meds, they won't be as bad." He shook his head when she started to protest. "You're not going to be able to sleep without them. Trust me."

She sighed. "I'm not going to win this argument, am I?"

"Is it really worth if it you spend an entire night laying here, miserable and cursing your stupid-ass pride?"

Another sigh, this one flirting with being downright dramatic. "No?"

"Good answer." He finally released her and shifted to face Theo. "This is a problem."

"Understatement of the century. Yes, Galen, this is a fucking problem." It wasn't Galen's fault any more than it was Meg's, but Theo couldn't seem to stop himself. "Someone pushed our girlfriend down the stairs." It struck him then of how it would look. The media would take one picture of Meg and start screaming that Theo or Galen was abusing her—maybe both.

He didn't say it. If he brought it up, they would both look at him like he was shit on the bottom of their shoe. He should be focused on Meg and solely Meg, but Theo had never been all that successful at turning off the part of his brain that schemed and planned and maneuvered. It was how he took care of what was his. Galen preferred to stalk a situation and take care of it privately—and permanently— but that wouldn't work this time.

They had no evidence to go on. There were half a dozen people off the top of his head who would happily see Meg gone, whether because she was a foreigner or because they blamed her for the unconventional setup of having two Consorts. If he'd just named Galen, they would have grumbled, but eventually Edward would marry and *his* children would take over the throne when the time came. The line would remain unbroken. And Galen's mother's family stretched back through Thalania's history nearly as far as Theo's did. His father might be Greek, but he had the right lineage to appease the Families.

Meg didn't.

Theo knew that when he named her Consort, but he'd been selfish. He wanted her, and he wanted Galen, and he wanted all three of them together. They *worked*, though not much seemed to be working in their current situation.

He couldn't send Galen hunting. Theo had no reason to doubt Galen would find the perpetrator, but he was no longer the head of security who could move through the background without drawing attention. He was Consort, and every move would be scrutinized down to the last detail.

Another sin to lay at Theo's feet.

"I'll take care of it." The words emerged before he had a chance to call them back. Theo climbed off the bed and yanked his shoes on. He tried to keep his emotions locked down, but they showed in his jerky movements.

"Theo—"

"I'll take care of it," he repeated. He took a slow breath and turned to face them, drawing from years of training to put a smile on his face. "Rest, princess. Galen will watch over you while you sleep. You're safe." Theo would do what it took to ensure she *stayed* safe. He picked up his suit jacket and shrugged into it. A quick check of the clock confirmed it was barely dinner time. Too late for what he had planned, but he'd make it work.

He felt Galen behind him as he stepped out into the hallway. "I have it covered."

"Funny you say that, because this whole situation is fucked." Galen grabbed his arm and spun him around. "We almost lost Meg and now you're running off alone? No. Fuck that. I'm not losing both of you."

He bit down on a sharp reply. Theo shot a look down the hall, but they were blessedly alone. He took Galen's shoulders and pulled him close, until their breath mingled and their soft words wouldn't linger for anyone to hear. "I'll take Isaac. I'm not rushing into anything."

"I don't know *what* you're not rushing into, Theo. You don't fucking talk to us anymore."

It hadn't been an intentional withdrawing. He simply saw how exhausted and stressed they were and tried to alleviate that in the only way he knew how: by not adding to it. Obviously he'd taken a wrong step somewhere, though that was a conversation for another day. *Add it to the growing list.* "Trust me this once, Galen. I'm going to handle this, and then we're going to sit down and figure some shit out. I promise."

Galen cursed and hooked the back of Theo's neck. He towed him in and kissed him, every move conveying fury and fear and a frustration he didn't know what to do with. Shit Galen would never say aloud, not where someone might witness it. Theo heard it all the same. He kissed his friend back, using tongue and teeth to reassure him in the only way he'd listen to. It wasn't enough. It wouldn't be enough until they got to the bottom of this, until they fixed the thing he hadn't quite managed to admit was broken.

Theo stepped back and Galen let him go. He nodded at the door. "Take care of her. I'll be back shortly."

"You're not going to tell me where you're going, are you?"

If he did, Galen might hogtie him and toss him into a closet, king or no. "Correct."

Galen cursed. "Tell Kozlov that if something happens to you, I'm going to hunt him down and gut him."

"I'll be sure to pass that information along." Theo hesitated, something soft and worried taking root in his stomach. "I love you."

"I know." Galen opened the door. "I love you, too. Don't do anything stupid."

"I wouldn't dream of it." He was about to go do something stupid.

Theo waited for the door to close and to hear the click of the lock being engaged. Then he went in search of his head of security, Isaac Kozlov. It didn't take long to track him down—the man took his job seriously and essentially lived in the hub where he ran the various security operations. He looked up as Theo walked through the door and lunged to his feet to bow, bending his huge body in half with more grace that he should have possessed with his size. "Your Majesty."

"Isaac." He closed the door behind him and checked the room. As usual, Isaac was alone. "I need you to do something for me, and both time and speed are of the essence." Back when Galen ran the security for the palace, he'd specifically recruited Isaac because of his unique skills pairing of being able to hack damn near any computer system, and being just as deadly as Galen was. There weren't many people Theo trusted beyond a shadow of a doubt, but Isaac numbered among them.

If only for his loyalty to Galen.

Isaac straightened. "Of course, Your Majesty. Is this concerning the Consort's attack?"

"It is." He hesitated. Once he pulled this proverbial trigger, there was no going back. "I need you to find Dorian Mikos."

5

Dorian Mikos drank his wine and watched the car approach the house. He already knew who it contained. He'd been warned several hours ago that an unknown entity had zeroed in on his location. Said entity may be unknown to his security team, but *he* knew exactly who had come calling.

His wife, Anne, leaned against the railing. She was beautiful, even after all these years, the wind teasing her blond hair away from her face. Age had burned away the youthful curves of her body, leaving only a sterling strength behind. She didn't look over. "He's early."

"Fear makes fools of even the best of men." Dorian wouldn't necessarily number Theodore Fitzcharles III among the best of men, but he brought more power to the table than most. He was a threat, and a large one. They'd spent six months watching him—watching all three of them —and considering their options. Thirty years ago, Dorian couldn't have imagined that his only son would be Consort to the King of Thalania. If he had, he would have played things out differently.

Impossible to hold sway over Galen when the man was as likely to shoot him as listen to anything he had to say. The boy really took things too personally. Power was the only god Dorian worshipped, and everything was sacrificial when it came to the long game.

Including his son.

He glanced over his shoulder at the black-clad man standing just out of earshot. "Send him up when he arrives." He waited for the man to nod and disappear before turning back to his wife. "We have to be careful with him. He doesn't function the same way Galen does." Their son divided up the world into black and white. It wasn't anything so simplistic as good and evil—it was the people who mattered to him and those who didn't. He might be moved to empathy for someone in danger, but he wouldn't compromise the people he loved because of a bleeding heart. It made him hellishly hard to manipulate because he was either apathetic or steamrolled over every perceived threat he came across.

Theodore, on the other hand, appreciated nuance.

One didn't come back from exile and ruin a perfectly good coup unless one was a threat.

Anne shifted, a signal that they were no longer alone. Dorian contemplated his wine and hid a smile. "What brings the King of Thalania to my humble home?"

He half expected the man to charge forward with accusations. Dorian should have known better. Theodore walked out onto the balcony and dropped into an empty chair. He picked up the bottle of wine and examined it. "Good vintage."

"I appreciate the finer things in life."

"Nothing but the best for you while you suffer out your

exile." Theodore made a show of looking around. "Suffering is a relative term, I suppose."

Dorian shrugged a single shoulder. "I suppose it is." He waited, but Theodore didn't seem interested in filling the silence. Dorian wrapped a stranglehold around his impatience. This was nothing more than a game of conversational chicken, and he'd be damned before he broke first and gave Theodore the upper hand.

Theodore leaned back and propped a foot on his knee, every inch the king at home in his kingdom. It didn't seem to matter that they weren't on Thalanian ground or that he currently sat in what amounted to enemy territory. "Phillip's doing well in prison. I know you were particularly concerned about your old partner in crime."

He blinked. Where was he going with this? "I'm not sure what you're implying."

"I'm not implying anything. I'm stating it baldly. My uncle, the one whom you conspired with to keep me from the throne, is doing well in prison." Theodore let both feet drop to the ground and leaned forward to brace his elbows on her knees. "I think it's time we had a discussion. Don't you?"

GALEN LAY in the dark and listened to Meg's breathing. Such a little thing—an inhale, pause, an exhale. He'd never put much thought into it before. Even after the car crash that had knocked Theo out and cut Meg up, he'd never really thought either of them would die. He'd been too focused on the end goal: finding and eliminating the threat.

This time, he didn't know who the threat was.

Someone had come into what amounted to their home and hurt their woman, and he was stuck here playing nursemaid while Theo went off and did... Whatever the fuck he was doing. Taking risks was supposed to be Galen's job. For so long, his entire purpose had boiled down to one prerogative—keep Theo safe. Six months wasn't enough to undo years' worth of thought process. He didn't *want* to undo it. No one was better than Galen was at keeping Theo from harm. Not even Kozlov, though he was at least mostly capable.

Galen closed his eyes, and immediately opened them again. There would be no sleep tonight, not with him counting Meg's every breath and listening intently for the door to open and Theo to return safely.

He should have gone with him. Watched his back.

But if he'd gone, who would have taken care of Meg?

Fuck, this wasn't his deal. He never bothered to be pulled in different directions, because his momentum had only one direction. Galen preferred to operate like that. Life was messy, as Meg was so fond of reminding him. Shit got tangled and emotions made them all act like damn fools. He loved Meg, and he wanted her safe. He loved Theo, and he wanted to keep his friend's ass out of danger.

Hours later, right as the first rays of dawn edged through the windows, the door opened. Even in the darkness, Theo appeared to have aged a decade. He ran his hand over his face and headed toward the bathroom. Galen could let him go, he could pretend to sleep and put off an uncomfortable conversation for a few more hours.

But then, Galen had never been the type to run from a fight.

He waited until the bathroom door closed, and then he carefully edged out from beneath Meg. A few seconds to ensure she was tucked in tight beneath the blankets, and then he stalked to the bathroom and slipped inside. Theo stood with his hands braced on the marble countertop, his head hanging loose between his shoulders. "I have good news and I have bad news."

"What's the bad news?" Better to take the hit head on instead of wasting the time bracing for it.

Theo didn't look up. "Your father is behind the attack on Meg. I don't have proof, but—"

"*Fuck.*" Galen strode to the shower and flipped the water on. The sound wouldn't completely mask their conversation, but Meg needed her sleep and with the pills in her system, she could wait to be looped in until she woke up. "Tell me you didn't do some fucking bullshit like seek Dorian out and talk to him."

Theo lifted his head and gave a wan smile. "We needed to know."

"If you needed someone to run interference, *I* am the appropriate option, you jackass. He's my fucking father, and I'm the only one who is guaranteed to be able to walk into his presence and back out again." Probably.

Theo finally turned to lean against the bathroom sink and crossed his arms over his chest. "That was true before. There's no reason to think it's true now." He hesitated the barest breadth of a second. "And, fuck, Galen, I know what seeing him does to you. I couldn't do a damn thing about it when I was exiled, but I can do something about it now. If that means I take on a little risk, then so be it."

"A little risk." Galen might laugh if he wasn't in danger of throttling his friend. "A *little fucking risk.*" He stalked closer. "Do you know what he does to people he has under his control?"

Theo's gaze flicked to Galen's bare chest, to the scars that marked his skin. "You know I do."

"You are the goddamn *king*, Theo."

"I'm aware." Theo grabbed his shoulders, the relative pain of his fingers digging into Galen's skin grounding him. He leaned in. "And if you think I'm going to let him near you if I have any other choice, you're a fucking idiot."

God, he loved this arrogant fool of a man. It didn't stop him from wanting to strangle Theo, but love and fear danced together in his chest, a confusing combination that had never been so strong as it was in that moment. "You took Kozlov."

"I took Kozlov and another three of his men that he trusts implicitly. They had a sniper set up before I ever walked into the house, and the entire meeting took place on the balcony."

Smart of Dorian. He wanted the King of Thalania's attention, and he'd ensured that nothing would hold Theo back from coming to him. It's what Galen would have done if he wanted to lay a trap, a spider sitting in the middle of a web of its own making. He sighed. He could keep arguing about this until he was blue in the face, but the end result was that Theo went, and now he was back. "Do not do that shit again, Theo. Promise me."

"No." Theo squeezed his shoulders. He looked away, and then back at Galen. "I know I've been fucking up. This balancing act is more difficult than I could have dreamed, and I know that you and Meg are things I have let slip that I shouldn't have. I can work to fix that, to make it right, but I can't do that if one of you is dead. If that means I have to do exactly what I did tonight a thousand times, then that's exactly what I'll do."

He could keep fighting this, or he could accept that Theo did exactly what Galen would have done if their situations were reversed. At the end of the day, it was no competition.

They had more important things to do than to fight each other. "Drama queen."

Theo gave a soft smile. "Only some days."

They stood there, so close their exhales mingled. It was the most natural thing in the world to lean in and take Theo's mouth. All of the bullshit, all of the back-bending and stressful days and politicking and shit Galen didn't want to deal with... It was all worth it because it meant he could do this whenever he damn well pleased.

Or at least it had been worth it until someone went after Meg.

Theo gripped the back of his neck and broke away enough to say. "Stop thinking and stay with me. Just for a little bit."

Meg was sleeping in the other room. There was nothing more they could do for her right now. More than that, *Theo* needed him right now. "Next time—"

"For fuck's sake, Galen, you're not normally one to talk something to death."

No, he really wasn't. "That's what you get for naming me Consort. Talking is all I do these days." He hadn't mean for the words to come out so bitter, but once they emerged, there was no taking them back.

For a second, it looked like Theo might kiss him again, but then he leaned back and released Galen. "I didn't know you'd hate it so much—either of you. I thought this was the only way we could be together."

There it was. Out in the open.

Galen crossed his arms over his chest. "We both know it wouldn't have mattered if you did. You want what you want, and to hell with anyone who gets in your way."

Theo narrowed his eyes. "Are you still pissed that I tried

to put you on a plane? I thought it was the best option at the time."

"Because you know best. I think we've more than proven that's complete bullshit."

"Fuck, Galen, what do you want from me?" Frustration roughened Theo's voice, the emotion reflected on his face. He ran his fingers through his dark hair and cursed again. "I don't know how to make this right. I don't know how to make *any* of this right."

Galen shook his head. What the fuck was he doing? They didn't need to hash this out. Things were the way they were. He might not have wanted the role of Consort, but he sure as hell wasn't complaining about sharing a bed with Theo and Meg every night. And being "out" in public made him realize how exhausting a couple decades' worth of sneaking around had been. He might not like that he had stepped into the exact type of role his father had always wanted for him, but that was his baggage. It didn't belong to anyone else.

He was on Theo before his friend had a chance to register the change. Six months of playing Consort hadn't made Galen into a wordsmith who knew the right things to say to get people to do what he wanted, and it sure as hell hadn't gifted him the skillset to comfort the two people he loved when they needed it. He didn't know if he'd ever play that part in their little threesome, but that was okay. Theo and Meg were better on both fronts.

This?

This, he knew how to do.

He took Theo's mouth, hard and rough and exactly what they both needed. The worst was yet to come for their current situation, and neither of them could do a damn thing about it tonight. But they could do this. He fisted the front of Theo's shirt and gave it a yank, scattering buttons across the tile floor. A quick flick of his wrist and he had Theo's belt free and his pants undone. Galen paused. They might not usually need words, but tonight wasn't like usual nights. "I know this clusterfuck is weighing on you. You don't have to bear it alone."

"I'm the king."

"You keep saying that. It's bullshit and you know it. You have us. You have *me*." He went to his knees as he shoved Theo's pants off. "You're going to do whatever the fuck you think you need to, and we both know it. Well, damn it, you'll take what you need from me tonight."

Theo reached down with a hand that didn't tremor in the least and ran his fingers through Galen's hair. "You think fucking is going to fix this."

"I think fucking is what you need to take the edge off so you can stop reacting and start using that impressive brain of yours to figure out a way through this shit." He took Theo's cock into his mouth before his friend could keep arguing. Galen had said his peace. That wasn't what this was about. Theo would do what Theo wanted to do. He always did.

And Galen would keep him anchored to the earth in the meantime.

He sucked Theo down. It didn't matter that Galen had Theo's cock inside his body more times than he could count. He never got tired of the full feeling, of having to stretch to compensate. Theo bumped the back of his throat and he relaxed into it, opening himself completely.

Theo held perfectly still for a moment, two, a third. Trying to hang onto that legendary control of his. His anger and fear and frustration were riding too close to the surface for him to win that particular battle. He cursed low and hard and then his hands were on either side of Galen's face, holding him in place as Theo started fucking his mouth. "This is what you want, you pushy asshole. You want me to fuck you until it hurts."

Yes.

If he did, maybe Galen would stop picturing Meg at the bottom of those goddamn stairs, her hazel eyes wide and unseeing, her chest still, her lungs having drawn their last breath. If Theo used him thoroughly enough, maybe he'd actually be able to sleep through what was left of the night.

Probably not, but it was worth a shot.

Theo picked up his pace, slamming into Galen's mouth. Into his throat. Involuntary tears sprang from his eyes, and Theo wiped them tenderly away without missing a single punishing stroke. "That's it, Galen. Take it all from me. Take everything." His words lost their carefully cultured tone, spilling between them, raw and true. "Drink me down. That's a fucking order." He came with a low curse, spilling over Galen's tongue and down his throat. He wrenched Galen to his feet and kissed him hard.

In that moment, they weren't King and Consort. They were just two men who had known each other most of their lives. There was perfect trust and perfect understanding.

Galen closed his eyes as a shiver worked through his body. He had to get control of himself. This shit wasn't him. "You have a plan."

"I have a plan." Theo hesitated, and then gave a rough laugh. "You're not going to like it."

That drew forth a laugh of his own. "When do I ever like your plans, Theo?"

"Yeah, well, you're really not going to like this one." He pressed a tender kiss to Galen's lips, and then ran a hand down his chest to cup his cock through his lounge pants. "Let's start a shower and take care of this."

"You're just trying to butter me up for some bullshit."

"Maybe." Theo was already turning away and moving to the shower. The muscles in his back stood out starkly against his skin. He'd lost what little color he'd gained during their exile, and he was almost as pale as Meg now. He glanced over his shoulder and raised a single dark brow. "Or maybe I just want the taste of your cock on my tongue to wash away all the bad shit that went down today."

Well, fuck. Galen couldn't argue with that logic.

He kicked off his pants and followed Theo into the shower.

6

Meg woke up far too early. Her shoulder ached and her face was one giant throbbing pain, but she refused to lay here and feel sorry for herself. Galen walked out of the bathroom as she climbed out of bed and pointed a finger at her. "I don't think so. Get back in bed."

"No." Normally, she would try to couch that under a reasonable tone, but she wasn't in the mood. Everything hurt and her patience was at an all-time low.

He growled at her, and she growled right back. Galen threw up his hands and raised his voice. "Theo, deal with her."

"Deal with me." She clenched her jaw and immediately regretted it. "I let you play nursemaid yesterday, because I know this whole thing freaked you the fuck out, but that stops now. I can walk, I can talk, and I'm not going to lie around and hide while you and Theo do whatever it is that you're planning."

His dark brows dropped. "Who's to say we're planning anything?"

"Don't patronize me."

"Fine. Fuck. Yes, we have some shit in the works." He ran a hand over his face. "Just stay safe until we can put it into motion." Galen ducked down and pressed a gentle kiss to the side of her mouth opposite her bruise. "I'll catch up with you later." And then he was gone, striding out of the room. Half a second later, a click sounded as the door shut behind him.

That hadn't gone how she'd expected. It hadn't gone how she expected at all.

Meg walked into the bathroom to find Theo shaving. He met her gaze in the mirror, his blue, blue eyes tracking the bruise that had taken over her face at this point. "I'd ask how you're feeling, but I imagine it's not well."

"You'd imagine right." She waited, but he went back to shaving. Meg frowned, irritated that she was irritated by him not jumping all over her like Galen had. "You're not going to order me back to bed, then?"

"Would it work if I tried?"

Damn it, she hated it when he was reasonable. "No."

"Didn't think so." Theo drew the razor over his neck. "I'm sure you have a perfectly justifiable explanation for why you're up and about instead of resting and healing."

Okay, maybe he wasn't going to be that reasonable. Meg lifted her chin and tried not to wince at the way her head spun. "Appearances matter." When he didn't immediately respond, she kept going. "Someone pushed me down the stairs yesterday, and if I hide in the room while you and Galen do whatever it is that you're doing, then it makes all three of us look weak. It makes *me* look weak. I'm already the foreigner and the one who keeps making mistakes when it comes to dealing with the nobles. If I stay in bed all day today, then they're going to think I'm running scared.

They're going to think they're halfway to winning... whatever it is that they're trying to win. No. Screw that. I'm not scared—I'm angry."

He finished shaving and set the razor on the edge of the sink. A quick wipe of the towel and he faced her. Meg rocked back on her heels. Even after all the time, the sight of him still knocked her for a loop. Galen was fierce and massive and scarred enough to mark his body as a warrior the same way his soul was. Theo's face was all sharp angles that somehow came together to create a masterpiece of masculine beauty. Vivid blue eyes and a mouth made for spinning sinful lies only ensured that he was a man who made people sit up and take notice. The first time Meg had ever seen him, standing in a VIP lounge above a crowded club, her breath had stalled in her lungs the same way it was now, as if she'd inhaled and simply forgotten to exhale.

God, she loved him so much, she didn't think her body could encompass the feeling.

"Meg?" He said her name as if it wasn't the first time.

"Sorry. You're just... you." She tried for a smile and abandoned it halfway through. Meg reached up and ran her hand along the smooth line of his jaw. "What did you say?"

"You don't have to do this."

"I know." And she did. If she let them, Theo and Galen would stand as her sword and shield against anyone who thought to hurt her. If she was a different person, she'd even consider it. "I can't let you fight my battles, Theo. Not even this one." Meg might be outclassed when it came to so many people who made their home here in the palace, but she'd be damned before she let them think her a coward.

He turned and kissed her palm. "I know." As if it was as simple as that. He knew she could stand on her own, so he didn't plan on arguing with her.

She might have appreciated the sentiment if it didn't make her so suspicious. "What are you two up to?"

"The plan isn't quite in place yet." He stepped back and moved to the closet on the other side of the bathroom. It was a massive walk-in with rows set out, each divided by who it belonged to. Theo's wardrobe took up an entire side, while Meg's rapidly growing dress collection competed with Galen's simpler black on black on black ensembles. Theo pulled on a pair of slacks and straightened. "Once I have the information we need to move forward, I'll loop both you and Galen in."

He trusted her to stand on her own, and he asked for her trust in return. Meg didn't want to be left out of whatever plans he intended to put into place. Theo had a habit of jumping first and figuring out if there was water on the way down. He always managed to land on his feet, but she feared that one day he wouldn't pull it off. In the end, she couldn't play the part of hypocrite. Not about this. "How long do you think you'll need?"

"Not long." He buttoned up his shirt and walked to her. Theo smoothed hair back and kissed her forehead. "A day, maybe two."

She could last that long. She *would* last that long. "Okay, I can do that."

"I love you, princess."

"Love you, too." She watched him walk out of the bathroom, unable to shake the feeling that something terrible was coming. It was more than the fact that she'd been attacked. Unfortunately, walking around with a bull's eye on her back seemed to go hand in hand with being with Theo and Galen. Some days she had more of a problem with that truth than others. This time felt different, though. It wasn't just prodding around the edges to find and exploit weak spots in their relationship. Whoever had shoved her hadn't cared if she lived or died. Those stairs were monsters. It would have been the easiest thing in the world to land wrong on her neck.

And that would have been that.

Meg showered quickly and managed to get her hair into a halfway decent ponytail despite how badly her shoulder ached. She didn't care. She was going to walk out of here and force everyone to look at what had been done to her. No reason to think the guilty party would react, but it couldn't hurt to stir the waters just in case.

She dressed in a simple pair of slacks, a deep purple blouse that complimented her nasty bruise nicely, and low black heels. The bed looked particularly inviting as she headed for the door, but Meg ignored its siren call. She meant what she told Theo—she wouldn't be the weak link. They needed to move forward as a unit, which was hellishly hard to do with Theo plotting in the background, but she could give him the couple days she promised him.

Meg opened the door and stopped short. Alys stood there, practically vibrating with worry. The smaller woman looked her over, her dark eyes wide and concerned. "Oh, Consort, you look terrible."

"Thank you, Alys," she said dryly. "I wasn't aware."

"Oh. I'm so sorry. I didn't mean it like that, of course. You look strong and sure." Alys held up her tablet almost apologetically. "Would you like your schedule?"

"Is Noemi Huxley on it?"

She blinked. "She did reach out and say she'd like to reschedule your tea whenever it convenient for you."

The last thing Meg wanted to do was have tea with Noemi while they sat around and talked about things that really didn't matter. But there was no ignoring the fact that the attack on her had come at a specific time. She'd been wandering the halls of the palace for six months without an incident. It was possible that the whole thing was a giant coincidence, but until she figured it out, she would operate as if it wasn't.

That meant she had to see Noemi.

"It's convenient for me now. Is she in the palace?"

"Uh..." Alys flicked her fingers over her tablet and clicked a few buttons. "It appears she is staying in the Huxley suites in the west wing.

Meg glanced at her watch. "I'll meet her in the informal dining room, the blue one." One of these days, she'd remember what every room in the palace was called, but since they numbered at well over a hundred and each had a specific name, Meg hadn't managed that feat quite yet. She'd been too occupied with memorizing the Families' lineage and how they were all interconnected with each other and with the throne. A tangled web that went back many generations. It was no wonder Theo had been so determined to take the throne. If the Fitzcharles line failed, Thalania would have a civil war on its hands. For all their politicking, no one actually wanted *that*.

Alys made an unhappy noise but her smile was perfectly professional. "Of course, Consort. Are you headed there now?"

"I am." She took a step and hesitated. "If Princess Camilla is available, I'd like to invite her to either lunch or tea."

"The King sent the princess to the country this morning."

Removing her from the line of fire. Smart. "In that case, cancel the rest of my appointments after Noemi and reschedule."

"Consort, you can't."

"I think you'll find that I can, and that I will." She'd spent so long being swept along with what she *should* be doing that she never took a step back to figure out if that was what she wanted.

Meg wanted Theo. She wanted Galen. That had been enough until now.

Maybe it was time to decide what she wanted as Consort.

She didn't know yet, but it damn sure wasn't to be scheduled from the time she woke up to the time she went to bed. She'd started to feel like a sideshow attraction, and the thought of spending the rest of her time in Thalania like that... No. She was done, and she was done today.

"But Consort... The schedule—"

Her new determination didn't mean she'd throw Alys under the bus completely. Meg strove for patience and turned to face her secretary fully. "Is there anything vital on the schedule today that absolutely can't be moved?"

Alys opened her mouth and seemed to reconsider. "Two things."

"Keep those and reschedule the rest." She headed down the hall. "Things are changing, Alys. Starting today."

IF NOEMI HUXLEY rushed to make it to breakfast, there was no evidence of it as she walked through the doors of the informal dining room. Her blond hair was done up in a series of braids that, on anyone else, would look messy, but on her just seemed chic. Her lipstick was even a pink that coordinated perfectly with her deep rose dress. Her smile died a terrible death when she caught sight of Meg. "Consort!" She caught herself almost immediately, moderating her tone and stopping her rush forward, but she couldn't quite recapture the easy smile.

She hurried over to the table and lowered her voice. "Meg, are you well?"

"Kind of a silly question, don't you think?"

Noemi made a face, the expression the first crack in her perfect presentation Meg had ever witnessed. "Yes, I suppose it is." She glanced over her shoulder and then marched to the door and shut it firmly. Another pointed glance at the camera situated in the corner of the room. "I would have thought that Mr. Kozlov would be taking his responsibility of keeping you safe more seriously."

Meg blinked. Of all the things she'd expected the other woman to say, a snippy comment aimed at Theo's head of security didn't number among them. "You know Isaac?"

"We're acquainted."

Which could mean anything from their having exchanged two words to their banging in supply closets every chance they got. If the palace even had supply closets. It was something Meg would have to investigate at some point. She tilted her head to the side, trying to picture it. Noemi was so... perfect. Obviously she couldn't be *that* perfect—she was human, after all—but she had just as much practice keeping the facade in place as Theo did.

Isaac Kozlov was... less so. For one, he was even bigger than Galen, and he wasn't attractive in the conventional sense of the word. Meg couldn't decide if it was because of his features—rough and carved with a brutal god's hand— or because he rarely smiled. The scar ringing his neck, thick and gnarled as if someone had attempted to garrote him, definitely didn't help matters.

"You and Isaac..." She gave herself a shake. "I'm sorry, it's none of my business." No matter how much the strange look on Noemi's face sparked her curiosity. "I actually asked you here so we could pick up where tomorrow should have gone."

Noemi took that in stride just like she seemed to take everything in stride. "Of course, Consort. I had arranged tea because..." She hesitated, her hands doing something resembling a nervous flutter in her lap. "I'm sorry. This just feels rather strange. We're adults, and we should be able to have a conversation like adults."

Meg wasn't sure whether the woman was aiming that comment at her or at herself. "Won't know if we can have a conversation like adults until you broach the topic you're dancing around."

"Right. Of course." Noemi gave herself a little shake and straightened her shoulders imperceptibly. "I get the feeling you don't like me much, Consort, and I'd like to know why."

Oh wow. Noemi was just full of surprises. Meg leaned forward and poured herself a cup of coffee. "Coffee?"

"Please."

She poured a second cup and watched as Noemi methodically doused it with several spoonfuls of sugar and a healthy dose of cream. Huh, she would have pegged the woman as fake sweetener and no cream. Apparently her people-reading skills as a former bartender were getting rusty. Meg waited for her to finish stirring before she spoke again. "Why does it matter whether I like you or not? Plenty of deals go down within these walls, and liking a person never enters into the equation."

"I'm aware." Noemi cupped her mug and inhaled slowly. "This sounds childish, and my father wouldn't thank me for saying it, but I had hoped we'd be friends."

Meg blinked. "Friends." Why in the hell would this

woman want to be friends with her? Surely there was some other element involved, some kind of manipulation. Meg had learned months ago that no kind overture came without some sort of strings attached, and this one couldn't possibly be the exception to the rule.

Maybe she's involved in whatever plot had me being shoved down the stairs.

Noemi gave a self-deprecating smile. "I know what you must think of me, but once upon a time Theo and I were quite close. I care about him and his happiness, and I would like to get to know you better. I had always thought he and Galen would..." She shrugged. "But I suppose they did, in a way."

"You knew about him and Galen?" As best Meg could tell, half the court had suspected something was going on, but Theo and Galen kept certain aspect of their relationship under wraps for the entirety of their adult lives... until now. Until Theo had come back for the throne and named both Galen and Meg as Consorts.

"I did." Noemi met her gaze steadily. "I'd like to know more about the woman special enough to matter to both of them. You've done a good job of keeping me at a distance, but it's rather exhausting not having anyone in the palace you can trust, isn't it?"

It was. She constantly felt like she was under attack—or surveillance, at the very least. There were times when she missed her best friend back home, Cara, so badly that she couldn't stand it. The only people she had to talk to without worrying about misstepping was Theo and Galen... and there were some conversational needs they couldn't meet. She missed having a friend.

That didn't mean Meg could trust Noemi.

Noemi nodded as if she'd responded. "I know. This place

is a cesspit of vipers, and you have no reason to believe my intentions are true. I'm sure plenty of the other noblewomen have sidled up to you with the intention of getting closer to the crown." Noemi made another face. "I'm not making a good case for myself, am I?"

"Not really." But Meg laughed. She couldn't help it. "Let me ask you a question."

"Of course."

"Why do you think someone pushed me down the stairs yesterday?"

There it was again, the shock that went all the way to Noemi's blue eyes. If she was faking her response, she was the best damn actress Meg had ever come across. Since Meg *couldn't* rule that out, she kept her expression even while Noemi worked through her surprise. "Someone *pushed* you?"

"Yes. Down the back staircase while I was on my way to tea with you."

"There are cameras." Noemi twisted to look at the one in the corner again. "Surely Isaac—Mr. Kozlov—saw the person who did it."

There it was again, that little slip of the mask. There was definitely something there beyond a casual acquaintance with Isaac. Meg filed that away to examine later. "They knew where the cameras were, and they avoided them. We're not even sure if it's a man or a woman."

"That's unfortunate." Noemi took a tiny sip of her coffee. "May I be frank with you?"

"I would prefer it."

"Okay." She nodded. "You could have been targeted for a number of reasons, but there are two options more likely than the others. The first is that the responsible party doesn't like that you're a foreigner and so close to the crown.

You have Theo's ear and, if you were an enterprising woman, you could use that influence to benefit both yourself and parties who aren't Thalanian."

Meg shook her head. "I would never."

"As I said, this is just potential motivation. The other option..." Noemi sighed. "The other option is that they either want to scare Theo back into exile—something that will never work—or they think that losing you will weaken him and make him more pliable."

She snorted. Theo being pliable was a laughable concept. "I think they'll find that reality doesn't match up to expectations."

"He's rather stubborn, isn't he?"

"Is water wet?" Meg finally picked up her coffee and took a long sip, letting the taste linger on her tongue. "If we're still being frank, I have no reason to trust you."

Noemi nodded. "You really don't. I wouldn't in your position."

Being what amounted to a princess was such a complicated affair, but in the end some of its skillset matched up with being a very good bartender. It was all about reading people and anticipating how they'd react in any given situation. In the pub back in New York, the worst she had to worry about was a bar fight or some drunk idiot getting handsy and having to be dealt with. Here, the stakes were so much higher. "Why help me?"

"Theo—"

"Yeah, you said that already. But if you and Theo were such great friends before all this began, he would act differently around you. He barely looks sideways at you, and it's not because I'm acting the part of the threatened, jealous girlfriend."

Noemi looked at her, *really* looked at her. "No, I suppose

you aren't." She sighed. "My father is the head of our Family. As progressive as Thalania is in many ways, the Huxley family drags behind the times. He won't give his blessing for me to take over operations. He intends to pass on the Head of Family title to my cousin instead."

Frustrating, but it didn't explain what that had to do with Meg.

Noemi nodded as if she'd spoken aloud. "I know this seems a small thing in comparison to what you've been dealing with since named Consort, but it's my life. My Family's life, even, since my cousin is a fool. If I had your support —support from all three of you—I could take the position before my father has a chance to give it away." She gave a tiny little smile that sent chills down Meg's spine. "Of course, the Huxley Family will remain a staunch ally to both Crown and Consorts for the duration of my time as Head of Family."

"Of course." Meg stared into her coffee. She had no business making these kinds of deals. She was...

She was Consort.

All this time, she'd felt like she was playing a role, a little girl in a princess gown and shoes she'd never manage to fill. If she was going to stay, if she was really going to do this, it was time to take charge of this little corner of her life.

She took another sip of her coffee. "I can't promise to do more than talk to Theo and Galen about supporting you." She continued before Noemi could speak. "But I will support your claim after you've enacted your coup." And she had a feeling Theo would as well. They needed allies. Several of the Families had come out in support of Theo, but it was more to hedge their bets than out of any real loyalty to him. Many of the younger generation of Families idolized him, and that would be useful in a few years, but the others saw his exile as proof that he wasn't infallible, and *that* was dangerous for everyone.

"Thank you, Consort."

She could let this stand, could keep the careful distance between them. Hell, she probably *should*. But since coming to Thalania, Noemi had never set off Meg's internal alarms the way some of the nobles did. She was beautiful enough to give a movie star a crippling case of insecurity, but Meg would have to be a particular brand of asshole to hold that against her. No, it was time to start putting down roots here. Real roots.

And that meant allowing for the possibility of friend-ship. "If we're going to be friends, you should call me Meg."

7

Theo spent the day getting everything into place. As King of Thalania, he could theoretically call any citizen he wanted to the palace, but the reality was that he had to tread carefully when it came to the Families. The seven noble Families could muster up a significant amount of power if they put their petty squabbles aside and focused on the throne, but they'd never bothered to try. With the attack on Meg, that may have changed.

Perhaps.

The problem was that he didn't know enough. Dorian Mikos was the puppeteer pulling someone's strings, but everything else lay shrouded in mystery. No telling who else intended to muddy their hands with Meg's blood, and certainly no telling their final goal. Civil war would serve no one in the immediate future, but there were members of the Families capable of playing the long game that numbered itself in decades instead of years. Occasionally even lifetimes.

He wouldn't know for sure until he forced them into the

light. Once he knew *who* Dorian was working with, he could take it from there.

He just had to play things painstakingly carefully in the meantime.

The door to his private office opened and he looked up as Galen stepped inside and shut the door behind him. He looked as tired of Theo felt, his shoulders drooping just the slightest with and the corners of his mouth pulled tight in what had become a permanent glare. A flip of the lock to ensure they wouldn't be interrupted, and then Galen stalked to the chair across from the desk and dropped into it. "This is a shitty ass plan."

"Yeah, you mentioned that last night."

Galen dragged a hand over his face. "It's not too late to change your mind. I don't like leaving you alone here— either of you."

He knew. Of course he knew. If Galen had his way, he would have bundled up both Theo and Meg at the first sign of trouble and left Thalania in the dust. Theo might be loyal to his country, but those two were only loyal to Theo. It was both an asset, and a danger.

For a moment, he let himself picture how it would play out. They'd take the tunnels from the palace into the city, where Galen would no doubt have a car waiting. A couple hours' drive would bring them to the border, and then across. They could be at Galen's home in Greece before the sun sank beneath the horizon the next night. There, nothing mattered but the three of them, and the only power plays they indulged in happened in bed.

Most importantly, no one would be trying to kill Meg.

It couldn't happen. To run now was the equivalent of going to his knees and offering his enemies his throat. All their throats. To protect her, he had to stay and he had to fight dirty while appearing untouchable. A difficult balance to handle, but he had Galen by his side. He'd had been playing dirty for as long as Theo had known him. The only reason Galen hesitated now was because he didn't like letting either of them out of his sight.

Theo leaned forward and braced his elbows on the desk. "Last night you told me I don't have to bear this burden alone. Have you changed your mind?"

Galen's dark eyes went flat and cold. "Don't you dare pull that fucking shit on me. I'm not some ass-kissing retainer who needs to be manipulated into doing what you want."

He wanted to indulge in harsh truths? Theo had more than his fair share to throw out like the weapons they were. "I need you to step the fuck up."

"What the hell did you just say?" Galen reared back like Theo had reached out and hammered an uppercut into his jaw.

"You heard me. I know you didn't want to be Consort. The whole damn country knows you didn't want to be Consort. You've spent the last six months brooding and throwing silent hissy fits every time you have to do something outside your comfort zone. Guess what, Galen? We're *all* outside our comfort zones in the current situation. This is bigger than us, as you were so fond of telling me when we were in exile. Or did that only apply when it was my sacrifices we were talking about?"

Galen shot to his feet. "Fuck you."

Theo shook his head, suddenly exhausted. Or maybe he'd never been anything *but* exhausted since taking the crown. Maybe if he and Galen had been out at that point as a couple...

No use thinking about it now.

He couldn't afford to display weakness, not even to

Galen. For this to have a chance at working, they needed the two-pronged plan he had formulated yesterday, and for that he needed Galen. People underestimated him, thinking that his size and brutality meant he was an idiot. Even though many of the nobles were scared of him, they would say things to him that they wouldn't say to Theo. Especially if they felt safe in their own territory and homes. If Theo could pull off this step alone, he would do it, but one of the many drawbacks of being king was that people were instantly on guard when he walked into a room. He could use that in most situations. Not this one.

Theo stood slowly. "Are you going or do I need to send someone else?"

"I'm going." Galen stalked to the door and yanked it open with enough force that it bounced off the wall and he had to catch it. "This is a fucking mistake, Theo."

"Possibly."

And then he was gone, striding out the door without looking back.

There were times when Theo took great pleasure in provoking Galen. His Consort was wound too tightly, and breaking through the carefully controlled exterior to the turmoil of emotions beneath brought him great joy. No longer.

He resumed his seat and got to work. Theo liked to take a portion out of his mornings and do the various paperwork that seemed to multiply overnight. He delegated things where he could, but he'd be a fool to pass off this responsibility entirely. Two of the Families were pushing hard for a new policy regarding their international relations and, while Theo agreed that Thalania's old policy needed to be reworked, he didn't like the direction they were headed. Better to temper it now than to run the risk of trouble later.

It all took so much damn *time.*

His office phone rang and he looked up to realize he'd been working far longer than he'd intended. No doubt someone was calling to gently remind him that he should have been somewhere an hour ago. He sighed and answered. "Hello?"

"Your Majesty, I..."

It took him several long seconds to identify the woman's voice on the other end of the line. "Alys? What's wrong?" *Where's Meg?*

Alys took a shuddering breath. "Your Majesty, I can't find the Consort. She's gone."

His heart dropped into his stomach. Meg couldn't be *gone.* She was in the middle of the goddamn palace, and there were hundreds of cameras around the property to ensure that something like this didn't just happen. For her to be attacked and then taken... *Stop that. You don't know what's happened yet.*

No matter the case, Alys wasn't one of the trusted few he'd allow his kingly facade to fall with. "Thank you, Alys. I'll take care of it." He hung up while she was still sputtering. Theo immediately called his head of security. "Isaac, find my Consort."

"Galen left a couple hours ago and boarded a chopper. The manifest is one you provided, so I'm assuming he's not the Consort you're talking about."

Theo closed his eyes and strove for patience, but there was none to be had. His mind kept up a chant of *find Meg, find Meg, find Meg* until there was no room for anything else. "Find Meg. Now."

"Working on it." Clattering in the background as Isaac works his magic on his computer. "Last seen heading into the west wing."

He opened his eyes. "The west wing is where the Families keep their suites."

"Yep." More clicking. "She's headed either in Huxley or Popov's direction. They both branch out of that particular hallway."

She'd had breakfast with Noemi Huxley this morning. Theo pushed to his feet. "Meet me there. Be discreet."

"Yes, Your Majesty."

Popov was a problem. He didn't think Lord Popov and his trio of sons were in the palace currently, but they had a habit of coming and going unexpectedly. None of them were particularly happy to see him on the throne, not when they'd been vocal supporters of Theo's uncle—and little brother. He didn't think Popov had the stomach for murder and abduction, but Theo wouldn't bet Meg's life on it.

Huxley? Huxley was a danger in an entirely different way. The man was a panicked beast, knowing the end was coming and fighting with everything he had to stay ahead of his fate. Theo would have guessed he was too concerned with outmaneuvering his daughter's ambitions to make a play for the throne, but stranger things had happened.

Noemi? Once upon a time, Theo and Noemi had been good enough friends that both their parents looked into the future and saw wedding bells, but it had never been like that between them. She was one of the few girls—and then women—whom he didn't need to pretend with. She'd always had her sights set on being the first female Head of Huxley Family, and marrying Theo would fuck that up. Considering he saw her as something between a sister and a friend, they were on the same page about their lack of shared future even back then.

Even if they hadn't been, he had found something he'd never dared to even dream of.

Happiness. Out in the open.

Granted, they were hardly living their perfect life at the moment, but they would get there. He'd ensure it.

Theo didn't quite run to the west wing, but he moved with a purpose that drove people out of his way, birds fleeing a coming storm. With each minute that passed, his mind helpfully supplied all the horrible things Meg could be experiencing. He'd thought they were safe for the next couple days, that the would-be assassin wouldn't strike again so soon.

Had he misjudged the situation again? The price of mistakes was too damn high right now.

Isaac Kozlov stepped out of a recessed door as Theo approached the hallway Meg had last been seen in. He was a giant bear of a man, big enough to make even Galen look small, and the wicked scar that wrapped his throat only made him more imposing. People didn't mess with Isaac unless they had no other option. Add into the mix that his technical skills made him the best head of security Theo had ever worked with and he was a force to be reckoned with.

None of that would help them now if something had happened to Meg.

Isaac fell into step next to him. "The only Huxley in the palace right now is Noemi. She wouldn't have done anything to the Consort."

Theo chose not to comment on that. It was obvious to anyone who paid attention that Isaac and Noemi had a history, but they weren't public about it and he did his best to respect that. Usually. There was nothing usual about their current circumstance. "All the same, we check Huxley."

"Yes, Your Majesty." His tight tone spoke of his displeasure over the order, but Isaac knew better than to argue.

They took the turn as one and headed for the Huxley suites. Years ago, the Families had thrown a collective fit about cameras in their wing of the palace. They claimed they were more than capable of protecting themselves, and effectively removed any responsibility for the palace to offer security. Theo's father had thought it a fair compromise at the time, but then neither Theo's mother nor his stepmother had ever disappeared into the west wing when her life was under threat. He regretted his father's capitulation now.

Theo reached for the door, but Isaac beat him there. He shot a look over his shoulder. "I got it." He banged on the door with a giant fist, the sound echoing down the hallway.

Ten seconds later—Theo counted—the door swung open and Noemi Huxley smiled at them. In all the years he'd known her, he'd never seen her less than perfectly put together, and this instance was no exception. Her long blond hair was pulled back from her face and she wore a vivid blue dress that set off her eyes.

Her gaze landed on Isaac first and a small line appeared between her brows. "Isaac?" The barest second, the truth lay in the air between the three of them, and then she'd recovered and her practiced smile was firmly in place. She turned pointedly to Theo, effectively dismissing Isaac. "Your Majesty. What can I do for you?"

"I'm looking for my Consort."

Her smile didn't flicker. "According to my father, the Consort is scheduled to visit our family home in the near future."

He liked Noemi well enough, but if she wanted to play games with Meg's life, he'd flatten her the same way he would an enemy. "Don't toy with me, Noemi. You know exactly which Consort I'm looking for."

"Yes, I know exactly which Consort you're looking for." She propped a hand on her hip. "The Consort is disinclined to see you at the moment."

Theo blinked. "Excuse me?"

"I do believe you heard me. Meg needed a break from all... this." She flicked her bright red nails at him. "I sent one of my people to distract Alys and Meg made her escape. I mean, really, Theo. How could you not know how close to breaking she is?"

He'd known. Of course he'd known. All three of them were a hair's breadth from fracturing, and the added pressure that came from their current threat level didn't help matters. That being said, he wasn't about to trust Noemi's word that Meg was safe. "Then it's obviously time for she and I to have a conversation."

"No."

"*No?*"

Isaac moved, stepping easily between them, his big back blocking Theo's view of the infuriating woman. "If the Consort doesn't want to see the King, then I'll ensure she's good."

A long pause, and Theo couldn't see their faces to know what passed between them. Finally, Noemi sighed. "I know a losing battle when I see one. Fine, Isaac. Talk to the Consort. And then you both will go." Another pause, shorter this time. "When she's ready to leave my room, I'll send for an escort."

When Theo had put together his plan, he hadn't anticipated on Meg reacting this way. She'd promised to give him a few days, but apparently that didn't mean she was going to sit quietly in the meantime. If he hadn't been so distracted, he would have known this was coming. Meg was never one to play damsel in distress, and she reacted to being hurt by coming back swinging. It was an impulse she'd wrestled mostly into submission in her time spent in Thalania, but the scare on the stairs would eliminate all the control.

Damn it, Theo really should have known better.

MEG DRANK her tea and listened to Noemi rip Theo a new one in the politest way possible. She made a few mental notes to use in the inevitable arguments she'd have in the future. Yelling her fool head off felt good sometimes, especially when Theo got particularly stubborn, but if she could get him to *sputter* the way Noemi had, that would be immensely satisfying. And worth the bottling up of her anger.

She wasn't angry now.

She took another sip of her tea. Okay, she could be truthful with herself, if with no one else. She was freaking pissed. It wasn't Theo's fault that she was hurt, and it certainly wasn't his fault that she was angry and scared and lashing out.

It was, however, his fault that he'd decided to take matters into his own hands and plan something and just expect her to keep going through the motions while he schemed. He'd told Galen what he intended—Galen was playing the part of minion in whatever it was, after all—but he'd left Meg out in the dark. Again.

Kind of difficult to consider herself a full partner in their little trio when the men shuttled her off to safety at the first sign of trouble, and didn't freaking *talk* to her about how they were going to deal with it.

So, yeah, Meg was feeling petty and pissed and not in

the least inclined to slow Noemi's little power play at the door.

Heels clicked on the tile and then the woman walked back into the room. If Meg hadn't already suspected there was something going on with Isaac and Noemi, she would have known it for truth in the blonde's stiff shoulders and tight mouth. She flicked a hand in Isaac's direction. "As you can see, she's hardly tied up and helpless."

"I see." There was a wealth of knowledge in those two words that didn't fit the situation. It would have been extremely uncomfortable, but he didn't aim it at Meg.

No, it was all for Noemi.

She marched to the brandy decanter situated in the corner of the room and splashed a healthy dose into a tumbler. "Run back to Theodore, Isaac. It's what you're good at."

Meg blinked. Oh shit, they were really going to do this in front of her. She cast a glance at the door. Maybe it wasn't too late to bolt. She could have her knock down drag out fight with Theo here and now. It was sooner than she wanted to, but at least she wouldn't have to sit as uncomfortable witness to... whatever was happening here.

Isaac turned away from Noemi and focused those cool blue eyes on Meg. "You're well, Consort?"

"Yes, I'm fine." She might have issues with Theo currently, but she wasn't about to take them out on his head of security. Isaac had scared the shit out of her once upon a time, but she'd grown to depend on him in the intervening time. He played an instrumental part of keeping them safe.

He failed yesterday.

That wasn't his fault.

Apparently no one had told that to Isaac, though. He went

down on one knee in front of her, his height meaning they were nearly eye to eye. "I'm sorry, Consort. I assumed the security within the palace would be enough to deter anyone who was up to no good, and I was wrong. You shouldn't have been hurt." His gaze traced the bruise on her face, as if in penance.

There were so many things she could say in response, but none of them would help. He'd decided it was his fault, and he'd go over the top to protect her moving forward so that he wouldn't fail again. Meg took a careful breath. "You're forgiven, Isaac."

"Not now. Not yet." But he pushed to his feet and gave her a deep bow that he usually reserved for Theo. "Please text me when you're leaving the Huxley suites so I can arrange an escort."

For all his guilt, she knew better than to push on this subject. If she did, he'd no doubt send someone to lurk outside Noemi's door to ensure Meg didn't slip away. Since she had no intention of slipping away—or being attacked again—she nodded. "I'm not going to rush around acting like an idiot just because I'm pissed at Theo."

He opened his mouth, seemed to reconsider what he was going to say, and finally nodded. "Thank you, Consort." He cast a glancing look at Noemi, but she was still putting entirely too much focus on the brandy. Finally, Isaac nodded again and walked out of the room.

As soon as the door clicked shut, Noemi took a shuddering breath and downed the entire glass of brandy. "God, that never gets any easier."

To ask or not to ask?

Really, it wasn't even a question. "What's going on with you two? There was enough tension in the room to cut it with a knife." Meg's people reading skills might be a little rusty, but even so she could see that there was history there. A whole lot of history.

"It's complicated." Noemi poured herself another glass and seemed to realize that she was doing a poor job of keeping her game face on. She walked back to the couch Meg sat on and perched on the other side. "If I was a different person, maybe there'd be a happy ending there, but..." She waved a hand at the suite. "I'm a Huxley. I can't leave my Family in the hands of my cousin, because he'll drive both our business and influence into the ground inside of five years. I'm the only one who can step into my father's role, and I already have things stacked against me without..." Another hand wave.

Simple enough to fill in the blanks. "Without falling for the hired help."

Noemi made a face. "That's a crude way of putting it. Isaac is more than the hired help. But no one else will see it that way, and my Family certainly won't. They won't follow me if I'm with him." She downed her second glass of brandy without a wince. "I have a duty, for better or worse. What is my happiness compared to the future of the Huxleys?"

"I don't have an answer for that." Theo had found a way around that very conundrum, but Theo was the King of Thalania, and his choice of naming two Consorts had made waves that they were still fighting their way through. Having both Meg and Galen at his side meant that his transition to take the throne was a rocky one at best, and that Families that would have given him their unconditional support now threw that choice into question.

Meg carefully slumped back against the couch. Her shoulder still ached something fierce and her headache would probably be with her until the day she died, but she was relatively free for the first time in six months. Her first day that wasn't scheduled out the ass and she wanted... "Do you like movies?"

Noemi raised her brows. "Are there people who exist who don't like movies?"

"Probably." Meg laughed. God, it felt good to laugh, to just...be. "Do you have anywhere to be today?"

Noemi perked up a little. "Are you suggesting a movie marathon?" She gave a brilliant smile. "I could order in junk food. I know they have it in the kitchens because Isaac—" She broke off and her expression clouded over for a few seconds before she shook her head. "Regardless, the kitchens keep a secret stock of junk food and I'm sure I could convince them to send us down some."

"That sounds like heaven." And it would serve the dual purpose of putting Theo in his place without Meg acting too stupid to live by running off to prove a point.

She couldn't pretend that was the only reason she wanted to hole up here. Every time she let her thoughts still, the imprint of the hands that shoved her down the stairs pressed against her back. Even knowing it was only a phantom of a memory did nothing to change the panic that fluttered in her throat at the memory.

She could have died.

She would have if the person who pushed her had their way.

What was more, Meg knew the thing Theo and Galen had very carefully not said since the attack. Whoever wanted her dead wasn't going to slink into the night just because they were foiled this time. They'd try again. They might be plotting to do exactly that right now. She shivered.

"Meg?"

Meg dredged up a half smile. "Sorry, just thinking dark thoughts."

Noemi's blue eyes went sympathetic. "Do you want to talk about it?"

"No, not really." She looked past the woman to the hall leading deeper into the suite. "I was serious about the movies if you were serious about the junk food." When Noemi didn't immediately move, Meg sighed. "I am freaked out. I'm trying very hard not to be, but I am, and I'm pissed at my men, but that's an entirely different issue. I'll have to talk this to death with them later after the little stunt we just pulled, and that's fine, but I really just want to hang out and not be Consort for a little while."

Noemi finally nodded. "How about this? Today you're not Consort, and I'm not a Huxley. We're just Noemi and Meg."

"Sounds like heaven."

"Good. You pick the movie. I'll call down to the kitchen."

8

A trip that was supposed to take two days instead took fucking *ten*. When he was twenty-six, Galen had done this tour as head of security, and he'd managed it in thirty-six hours. Speak with the Head of Family, get the information he needed, get out. Apparently that wasn't an option as Consort. When he walked through Family Vann's door, they must have started a phone tree, because every other Family anticipated his arrival and drew it out. They insisted on wining and dining him, on dodging his questions, on grilling him about policies Theo was considering. Oh, they wouldn't call it anything as harsh as *grilling*. Questioning, polite and persistent, until he wanted to start smashing things. To make things even more complicated, the Families that had made snide comments about him being a traitor's son when he was sixteen now practically bowed and scraped to avoid pissing him off.

He shouldn't have liked it.

Power was never Galen's goal.

Safety and stability, yes. Power, no.

His helicopter landed just outside Huxley Manor,

kicking up wind strong enough to stagger the party of waiting people. Huxley himself numbered among them, which made Galen's job that much easier. He clasped the pilot on the shoulder. "We have enough fuel to get back to the Ranei?" The capital city was only an hour away by air.

"We refueled this morning before leaving Lady Nibley's residence. We're good to go when you are."

"Don't wander. This won't be a long visit." Theo kept assuring him that things were under control at the palace, but the thread in his voice made a liar out of him. Something was going on, and he didn't want Galen to know about it. Since this chore *had* to be done, Galen swallowed down his need to fly immediately back to the palace and did his duty.

That didn't mean he was going to led Lord fucking Huxley slow him up. Ten days was eight days too long, and he was finished with this goddamn chore.

"Yes, Consort."

He removed his headset and climbed out of the helicopter. Lord Huxley tried to speak over the rotating helicopter blades, but Galen shook his head. "Inside." If they stood screaming at each other on the lawn, it would draw out this conversation. He didn't wait for Huxley to agree. He just walked past the red-faced man and up the stairs leading to the front door.

Inside wasn't much better. When Huxley had taken over as Head of the Family, he'd renovated the place, tearing down anything that reminded him of his parents. Though Galen could appreciate the sentiment, the result was a gaudy display of wealth that set his teeth on edge. Galen was technically a lord in his own right, with a substantial income that Theo's wizardry with the stock market had turned into truly outstanding. Beyond that, he'd been raised in the palace alongside Theo since he was sixteen. Displays of wealth didn't intimidate him.

It wasn't *intimidation* that made him compare Huxley to a stray dog who needed to piss on everything to prove he had the biggest dick in the room. From the over-the-top veins of gold in the marble beneath his feet to the massive painted—fucking *painted*—portrait of Huxley himself situated over the entrance, it was enough to give Galen heartburn.

I'm only here to deliver a message.

He turned to Huxley, but the man was already moving deeper into the house. "Coffee?" He didn't give Galen much choice, disappearing down the hall and leaving a pair of nervous-looking women in honest-to-God maid uniforms fluttering behind him like discarded trash. They glanced at each other, at the hall, and at Galen, as if not sure where they were supposed to go.

He decided for them. Galen stalked after Huxley. The man knew why he was here. The Families' information network was nearly as good as his own. The only reason he'd surprised Lady Vann was because Theo hadn't given anyone notice—even the pilots—before he'd sent Galen on this little trip.

Huxley led him into a sitting room that was just as ostentatious as the parlor had been, from the gold leafed frames around all the paintings to the priceless antique table Huxley used to prop his feet on after he sat on one of the chairs. "What can I do for you, Consort?"

Galen didn't bother to sit. He wouldn't be here that long. There were Families he had to cater to and kiss ass with. Not this one. Huxley had all but announced his determination to see Theo's downfall at the coronation. No reason to pussyfoot around as a result. "His Majesty requests your presence at the palace in two days. He's very grateful for the support of the Families in this time of transition and would like to honor you in thanks." The words rolled off his tongue without the least bit of irony. It was the fucking Families fault that Theo taking over the throne had been rife with challenges and stupid, petty bullshit. Theo thought it was his exile causing the problems, but Galen knew the truth— he hadn't played their game and married a suitable noble-woman with the right bloodlines. Instead, Theo had named Galen and Meg as Consorts. A man who was half-foreigner and son of two traitors, and a woman who was *all* foreigner.

Yeah, the Families had a collective fit as a result.

But calling them on that bullshit was strictly forbidden, so here Galen was, smiling tightly and delivering lies with an ease he'd never been able to accomplish before now.

Huxley sat back and pulled on the edge of his mustache. "This wouldn't have anything to do with your Meg's acci-dent, would it?"

Keep her name out of your fucking mouth.

Galen fought to maintain his calm expression. "How could it, when it was an accident?"

"Hmmm." Huxley twisted his mustache, a nervous gesture that would have lost him a fortune in poker. "Would you indulge an old man in a question that's not particularly politically correct?"

Here we go. Galen motioned for him to continue, but he braced himself against giving away any reaction.

"Why her? She's pretty enough, I'll grant you that, but she's a bit of a bitch, and she doesn't know how to play the game." Something must have slipped past his control because the older man rushed on. "If you needed a woman who could handle both of you, my Noemi is more than capable, and she brings a bloodline that will please the

Families in the process. Naming her as Consort instead of the foreigner would all but assure that the roadblocks the king has been dealing with disappear."

So that was their game.

Replace Meg with someone more suitable to their interests.

It shouldn't have surprised him that the Families were more than happy to whore out their daughters to play third to Galen and Theo as long as they wedged their way up the political ladder. The knowledge still sickened his stomach. The only god these people worshiped was power, and the lengths they went to in order to claim the slice they considered their own...

Fucking unforgivable.

Galen walked to the side table and picked up a heavy crystal candlestick, examining it as he gave himself time to smother his reaction. Beating this piece of shit over the head might give him temporary pleasure, but it wouldn't get to the heart of the problem. They had no way to tell if Huxley's grand plans were linked with Dorian's—or if the old man just saw an opportunity and refused to let it pass.

Either way, Galen wouldn't forget.

"Have you talked to your daughter about this proposed arrangement?" His voice sounded distant and uninterested, completely unlinked to the maelstrom of fury rising with every inhale. He had to get out of here, and quickly, but he wanted what answers he could find first.

"Noemi is a good girl. She does what's best for the Family."

Which meant everything and nothing. Noemi could be a stone-cold bitch when it came to seeing the Huxley Family interests advanced, and that might even include taking a position as Consort. It would put her in a unique position to influence Theo to support policies that benefited the Huxleys. Whether that was part of her plan or not remained to be seen, but Galen wasn't taking any chances. "I'll convey your offer to Theo." He turned to the door. "Be at the palace in two days, Lord Huxley."

"Oh, I'll be there. I wouldn't miss it for the world."

With those words ringing in his ears, Galen strode out of the house and back to the waiting helicopter. The entire trip back to the palace, he ran Huxley's words—and their implications—through his mind. Whether or not Noemi was part of Huxley's plans didn't matter. The fact that they couldn't trust her *did*.

He barely waited for the helicopter to set down in Ranei to head for the palace. Kozlov met him at the door, and the big man held up a hand before he got a word out. "The King is in his office. The Consort is in Noemi Huxley's suite."

Christ, she moves fast. He'd known Noemi was circling Meg, but he'd chalked it up to the normal politicking. He couldn't keep doing that with Huxley's words ringing in his ears. If Noemi was in on this plot, she wouldn't be so stupid as to harm Meg while they were alone together.

That didn't stop Galen's rage from rising with every beat of his heart.

"Not for long." Galen picked up his pace, and his expression must have been as thunderous as he felt, because people scattered out of his way as he stalked the halls. Thank god it was late enough that there weren't many or he'd be hearing from someone pissed about his breach in decorum tomorrow.

It took nearly ten minutes to reach the west wing. Ten minutes too long for his peace of mind.

Kozlov registered his intention the second he hit the door and charged through. "Goddamn it, Mikos!"

Galen wasn't listening. He wouldn't be listening until he set eyes on Meg and assured himself that she was okay. Safe. No one was in the sitting room just inside the door so he followed the sounds of the television deeper into the suites.

"This is a mistake, Mikos." Kozlov grabbed his arm. "You're fucking up."

Galen twisted just enough to stare at the man's hand touching him until Kozlov released him. "I didn't ask for your opinion."

Kozlov stepped back, his eyes going hard. "Fine. Your funeral."

Galen walked into the living room to find Meg and Noemi sitting curled up in their respective fuzzy blankets, an array of packages in front of them of cookies, chips, and candy. Noemi saw him first and started to stand, but he pointed at her. "Sit."

"Excuse me?"

He ignored her and turned his attention on Meg. She looked much the same she had ten days ago, though her bruise had faded significantly in the time apart. "We're leaving."

She gave him a long look, and then treated Kozlov with an identical one. "My movie isn't finished."

"Over my shoulder or on your feet, Meg. Your choice, but we are leaving right this fucking second."

She seemed to consider his words—and whether she wanted to fight them—but finally sighed. "He's going to be difficult."

Noemi snorted. "Honey, I think we passed difficult months ago."

Meg pushed to her feet and wobbled a little. She pointed at Galen. "Stand down. I'm not exactly happy with you right now, and if you push this, I'm going to make a scene."

"My shoulder or your feet," he repeated.

"Touch me and I'm going to kick your ass." She turned and gave Noemi a little wave. "See you tomorrow?"

"I wouldn't miss it for the world."

She'd be alone with Huxley's daughter again over his dead goddamn body, but this wasn't the time or place for that argument. Until they knew which side of her father's ambition Noemi landed on, Meg wasn't going anywhere near her. He marched Meg into the hallway and didn't wait for Kozlov to join them before he pressed his hand to the small of her back and started for their rooms. They were on the opposite side of the palace, creating far too much opportunity for silence.

Naturally, Meg wasn't having any of that shit.

"I don't know what horse you rode in on, but that was bullshit. You have to know that was bullshit."

He didn't look at her, too busy scanning each cross-section of hallways for a potential threat. "You can't trust Noemi Huxley."

"No, really? I can't trust anyone in this place. *That's* been made more than clear these last couple months."

"Anyone except us."

Meg stared straight ahead. "I stand by my first statement."

All the bottled-up emotions he'd been fighting the entirety of the day bubbled up in his chest. He couldn't take it anymore. Galen didn't do secrets any better than he did politics. Yeah, he wasn't an open book for anyone who bothered to look, but he didn't actively kept things from the people he cared about. He sure as fuck hadn't wanted to start like this.

He looped an arm around Meg's waist and towed her through the nearest door. It was one of the endless sitting rooms the palace hosted. The one's decorations went back to one of Theo's great-grandmothers, though Galen couldn't begin to guess the name of the woman pictured atop a horse in the black and white photo dominating the one wall. She didn't matter. Meg did.

He shut the door and locked it, and then turned to face her. "Get it out."

"Excuse me."

"You're pissed. That's fine. You can be fucking pissed and we can fight until we both get tired of it, and then we can fuck out the rest of your frustration. But you don't get to pretend that you can't trust me—or Theo. That's a goddamn lie, and you goddamn well know it."

Meg spun on him and got right up in his face, an impressive feat considering he had a good eight inches on her. "Fuck. You. And fuck Theo, too, for that matter. *Ten days*, Galen. You've been gone for ten fucking days and no one thought to tell me that your 'little errand' would run longer than a week. You and Theo and your goddamn plans—"

"It was necessary."

"That's what he said." She cursed and cursed some more. "I get that I'm outmatched when it comes to literally everything connected to Thalania, but you two are acting like I'm a kid who can't be told the scary thing because I can't handle it. That's not fair, Galen." She took a step back, glaring. "And don't you dare tell me that life isn't fair. *You* were the one who promised open communication, and now you've both shut me out."

"It's not like that."

"Really? Then tell me what it's like."

He should wait until all three of them were together. This was Theo's grand plan, not Galen's. Apparently he hesitated too long because Meg's expression shut down. He could actually see the walls going up behind her hazel eyes. She took another step back. "Yeah, I didn't think so."

"Meg—"

"Shut up." She recovered the three steps to him and kissed him. Surprise stilled him faster than if she'd sucker punched him. Meg drew back enough to say. "Just...stop talking unless you're going to be growling filthy things in my ear. I'm mad at you, and I'm wound up, and I feel like I'm about to come out of my skin."

He cupped her ass, drawing her flush against him. She immediately rolled her hips, grinding against his hardening cock. *Fuck.* He tightened his grip, trying to hold onto reason. "You're hurt."

"It's been *ten days*, Galen. My shoulder is fine. My face looks worse than it feels now." She rolled her hips again. "And let's be honest. It wouldn't be the first time you've fucked me while I'm hurt, and with the way things are going, it won't be the last." She nipped his bottom lip hard enough to send pain sparking through him. "Fuck me, Galen. We can keep fighting once we're back in the rooms with Theo."

He couldn't resist her now any more than he'd been able to resist her the first time. "Bend over the back of that dainty couch and pull your dress up, baby. Let me see you."

THERE WAS something wrong with Meg. There had to be. Maybe it was a wire crossed wrong or some chemical imbalance, because every time she got pissed at one of her men, she ended up kissing him, which resulted in truly outstanding fucking. Orgasms were good. They were great, even.

Orgasms just didn't solve the thing they'd been arguing about to begin with.

She had a moment of wondering if she should bolt for the door... wondering if Galen would chase her through the halls.

He would. She knew it down to her very soul.

Just like she knew that someone would witness it, and the resulting scandal would make all three of their jobs harder.

Meg set the fantasy away. They were going to play out a different one right now, and maybe she'd get some answers at the end of it. If nothing else, she'd reclaim the distance Galen's absence had put up between them. Banish the worry and sleepless nights with his side of the bed empty, wondering if he was safe and when he'd come home.

She knew what Galen wanted—her bent over with her dress up around her hips—but Meg wasn't in the mood to obey. Instead, she pulled the shift dress over her head, and dropped it on the ground next to her feet. Her panties and bra followed, leaving her only in her heels. She cast a quick look around the room and decided on the low-backed chair instead of the couch. Meg walked to it, conscious of his gaze pinned to her ass, and leisurely leaned over to prop her elbows on the back of the chair. The position left her head lower than her ass, and she spread her legs a little to give him a show.

"You don't follow instructions worth a damn." His tone roughened to something resembling a growl.

Got you. Meg tilted her hips up a little. "I don't hear you complaining."

"How could I when the view is so damn pretty?" His voice was closer this time, though she hadn't heard him move. For such a big man, Galen was as quiet as a cat when he wanted to be. "Spread your legs wider."

She obeyed. Maybe she should have fought him harder, made him work for it more, but Meg was all about results. And she wanted Galen's hands on her body, his cock deep inside her, his words rolling through her until all her stresses and fears disappeared. Until there was only him and the pleasure he dealt her.

He went to his knees and then his hands were on her, running up her thighs to part her pussy with his thumbs. "There you are. It's been days, baby, and I know you're feeling neglected and pissy because of it, but I'm going to take care of you right here, right now. I won't stop until your legs are shaking and you're muffling your screams on that ugly ass chair you're clutching."

Meg bit back a laugh. "Talk is cheap."

"Mmm."

She loved it when he made that pleased sound. It never failed to roll down her body and curl her toes. Meg fought to keep her voice vaguely disinterested. "And are you talking to my pussy, or talking to me? Because—" He dragged his tongue over her, stealing the words from her lips. "Oh."

"Yeah. Oh." He urged her legs wider yet and shifted to roll the top of his tongue over her clit. "You taste good, baby. Eager. Like you're going to fuck my mouth if I don't get you there fast enough." His breath over her clit sent a wave of goosebumps rising over her body in anticipation.

Focus, Meg. You give in now and he wins.

Considering Galen winning looked like his mouth all over her, it wasn't the most convincing of arguments. "Maybe I will. Or maybe I'll just reach down and finger myself because you're taking too damn long."

"Do it." He nipped the curve of her ass hard enough to make her jump.

She released the chair with one hand and winced, the move pulling at her shoulder. Meg barely had a chance to curse her pain before Galen picked her up and tumbled her onto the couch. He took up position between her thighs and hooked one of her legs over the back of the couch, spreading her wide. "Better."

It was, but she refused to admit as much. Meg coasted her hand down her stomach and stopped just short of her pussy. "Wait."

"You're trying my patience."

Yes, she was. She really, really was. Meg gave him a cocky grin. "Show me yours and I'll show you mine."

"I've got you spread so wide, I can see every bit of you." To demonstrate, he dragged a finger down her center.

"Take out your cock, Galen. Having it stuffed into those slacks can't be comfortable." She eyed the impressive bulge in the front of his pants and threw his own words back in his face. "Let me see you."

He didn't hesitate. His dark eyes flared hot as he dragged down his zipper and shoved his pants down enough to free his cock. Galen gave himself a rough stroke. "Okay, baby. Let's play your game. How long can you hold out?"

"Longer than you." She dragged two fingers through her wetness and up over her clit. She was already so turned on, Meg wouldn't last long like this, not with Galen braced over her, jacking himself and looking at her like she was both heaven and hell to him.

"Your tits are looking neglected. Pinch those pretty pink nipples for me."

Meg kept stroking her little circles as she reached up with her free hand to obey his command, rolling first one nipple and then the other between her fingers, until they were aching and needy for his mouth. The air between their bodies went charged and hot. It shouldn't be so sexy that the only place Galen touched her was his clothed thighs helping urge hers wide, but it was. "If Theo could see us now..."

"Who says he's not watching?" He glanced up, and she followed his gaze to the camera situated in the corner of the room.

The one with the clear view of both their bodies from their current position.

That was all it took. Meg came, her orgasm sweeping through her with gale-force wind. The strength of it bowed her back and drew a cry from her lips. Galen followed seconds later, coming across her stomach, marking her as his, if only for that moment. Silence fell across the room, only broken by their harsh breathing.

Finally, Galen dragged off his shirt and cleaned her up. "The camera's off."

Meg blinked. "What?"

"People fuck in these rooms more often than anyone realizes. While security notes who's screwing who and take a few screenshots to back the information up, they aren't in the habit of filming porn. As soon as it was apparent what we were doing, the camera clicked off.

"Oh." She flopped back onto the couch, not sure if she was relieved or disappointed in that revelation. "Okay."

Galen saw. The ass always seemed to see the thoughts kicking around inside her head. "You want to be filmed? We can make that happen. But not for those fucks in the security hub. The only people who are going to be watching me or Theo pound that pretty pussy of yours is *us*." He stopped and looked at her, hard, his dark brows drawing down in consideration. "Unless you want a full audience?"

Meg let herself think about it for half a second and shuddered. "Pass. My extrovert tendencies only go so far as being watched by one of you."

"If you change your mind—"

"I won't."

Galen gave her another long look. "It's our responsibility to meet your needs, Meg. Whatever those needs are. I know we've been doing a piss poor job of it lately, but that doesn't change the truth of it." He pulled her gently to her feet. "Come on. We still have a castle to storm and a king's ass to kick."

"I'm still not happy with you."

"I know, baby. Trust me. I know."

9

Theo knew what kind of night it would be the second the door slammed open. Meg marched into the room, her cheeks flushed and her hair tangled, only further confirming what had delayed Galen after he arrived back in the palace. The man himself walked through the door after her, his shirt untucked and all expression wiped from him face.

Most of the nobles thought Galen was one step off a robot at best, and a broody son of a bitch at worst. Those assumptions couldn't be further from the truth. Galen simply had better control than most other people. The fact he'd bothered to layer in his control meant he was keeping something bottled up that would bite them all in the ass if left to fester. Galen shut the door and threw the lock. "Meg."

"No. Orgasm or not, I'm still pissed at you—at both of you." She barely looked at Theo as she headed into the main bedroom and kept going. "I'm taking a shower. You have ten minutes to figure out if you're going to keep pulling this macho bullshit where you don't tell me what the hell is going on or if you're going to pull your heads out of your asses." She opened the bathroom door and glared at them over her shoulder. "Here's a hint—there's only one right answer." She disappeared and shut the door softly behind her.

Theo glanced at Galen. "Which of the sitting rooms did you despoil this time?"

"Fuck off." When Theo just stared, he growled. "The one with the horse-loving great-grandmother."

"Ah, Bernice Fitzcharles. From all accounts, she was one of the more difficult queens."

If anything, Galen's gaze flattened. "The history lesson is not required." He tossed his balled-up shirt in the general direction of the trash. "The Families will be here in two days."

"Thank you."

"Don't thank me. You didn't give me a goddamn choice in any of this." He glanced at the closed bathroom door, behind which they could hear the shower running. Given Meg's predilection for eavesdropping, Theo didn't argue when Galen moved back into the sitting room and lowered his voice. "Huxley showed his hand. He wants his daughter in Meg's place."

Theo blinked. "He wants *Noemi* to be our third?"

"He seems to think that the Huxley bloodline will smooth away a lot of the negative reactions to how unconventional our arrangement is."

Huxley wasn't wrong in this case. The Families were nothing if not consistent, and they wanted their interests seen to. Having one of them in close proximity to the throne would calm feathers ruffled by so many foreigners attached to Theo.

Fuck. He should have seen that as a possibility sooner.

Theo dropped into one of the chairs and ran his hands

through his hair. "Does he honestly think that throwing Meg down a set of stairs is going to be enough to drive us into yanking the first available woman into bed with us as a replacement?"

"Considering how often he fucks around on his wife, yeah, I think that's exactly what he believes."

He cursed. They'd known something was going on and Meg was the target but *this?* This was fucked up beyond all reason. Huxley might believe that they would just replace Meg with a little time and motivation, but Dorian was too smart for that. He knew better. The question remained— were they working together? Or was Huxley simply looking to capitalize on the attack after it happened?

Realization washed over him, leaving a cold that wormed its way right down to his center. "She's been spending significant time with Noemi all week."

"Yeah, apparently she has. Something you forgot to fucking mention when we talked while I was gone." Now Galen let the anger burn through. He shoved himself into motion, pacing the sitting room in a handful of furious strides. "We can't tell her to avoid Noemi."

Theo snorted. "Good luck trying to get that to stick."

"Or, here's a novel idea." Meg stepped through the doorway, her hair wet and wrapped in a towel. "You could just stop whispering about it and talk to me like I'm an equal member of this triad."

Shit. He should have seen that coming a mile away. Theo pushed to his feet. "Princess—"

"No. Now is not the time for pet names and pacifying me. You of all people should know that." She looked from him to Galen and back again. "You're treating me like a child."

"You're acting like a brat," Galen fired back. "We know

the ins and outs of this shit better than you ever will. Can't you just throw us a fucking bone and trust us for once instead of questioning everything to death?"

For fuck's sake. Theo started to turn to tell his friend to stand down, but Meg was there, getting in Galen's face. "Trust goes both ways, *baby*. You can't package me up in bubble wrap to keep me safe."

"No, but I sure as shit can ship your ass back to New York."

"That is *quite* enough." Theo stepped between them and used his shoulders to muscle them away from each other. "You." He pointed at Galen. "Walk it off. Shower or run or find a drink, but don't come back here until you can be helpful and stop swinging your dick around."

Galen stared at him a long moment, his expression reflecting the same toxic mix of emotions bubbling up inside Theo. Fear. Anger. The need to smash their enemies to pieces. And then, just like that, he blinked and it was gone. "Sure, Theo. I'll go. But if you don't have a solution by the time I get back, then I sure as fuck am going to do what's necessary."

Child's play to read between the lines. *I'll take out Dorian.*

It wouldn't help. Their enemies' plans were too far along now, and too widespread. Neither Dorian nor Huxley had shoved Meg down the stairs. "Go."

"Consider me gone." He stalked to the door and slammed out of it.

Theo finally turned his attention to Meg. "That was shitty of you."

"Excuse me?"

"You heard me. You know how he operates, and you know that his first instinct is to protect. It's driving him crazy that he wasn't there to stop what happened to you, and driving the bone in his throat deeper was shitty of you."

Meg drew her brows together and poked his shoulder. "I'm sorry, did *you* get shoved down some stairs? How is it my responsibility to tiptoe around Galen's emotional shit?"

He rounded on her. "The same way it's our responsibility to tiptoe around *your* emotional shit, princess. You think I don't know how crazy it makes you living in the palace? That it eats away at you thinking that you think you depend on me for your safety and the shit you own. That you believe your independence is gone."

"Because it is!"

"Fuck that."

She shoved her hands through her hair and then winced when the move seemed to pull at her injured shoulder. "I guess I missed the part where I did a single thing to earn this life except ride your dick like a champ."

God save him from the two stubborn ass loves of his life. "You're titled."

"Excuse me."

"It came with being Consort. You have your own home in the southern providence. It actually borders Galen's lands, but that was just a happy coincidence. You've been bringing in an income this entire time."

She looked at him like she might strangle him on the spot. "That's not mine."

"Actually—"

"It's *not mine*, Theo. It's something you can take away, and so it's not mine. I get that you don't understand that, but at least try to pretend that you aren't going to keep putting money away in my account like I'm some kind of paid mistress."

His patience bottomed out. "You're not a mistress, Meg.

You are Consort to the King of Thalania. Time to stop acting like it's a fucking temporary position." How could the two people he loved most in this world be so goddamn infuriating?

Theo had spent his life preparing for the stress to run a country and have the lives of millions depending on him, at least in part. All it took was a single conversation with Meg and Galen to have him yelling his fool head off.

"That's enough of that." He turned away from her and stalked into their room to the phone on the wall.

"That's enough of that? Do you even listen to yourself when you talk, Theo? I'm not one of your subjects. You can't just decide to be done with a conversation because you're tired of it."

He knew that. Of course he knew that. But this conversation, while valid, wasn't really about Meg's issues with leaning on anyone as much as it was about their mutual fear about what might happen in the future. The enemy was at the gates, and despite everything, they'd been caught flat-footed.

But they couldn't take a step back and focus until they lanced this particular wound. Something impossible to do in the palace with the constant reminder of both the threat and their new respective positions. "We're not done with the conversation, but we aren't going to continue it here."

"What the hell are you talking about?"

Theo grabbed the phone and dialed Isaac's extension. Unsurprisingly, the man was still awake. "Yes, Your Majesty?"

It didn't matter how many times Theo told him to use his first name, Isaac refused to do it. He bit back a sigh and ignored Meg staring daggers into the side of his head. "I need transportation set up for myself and the Consorts.

Something subtle. We're taking an overnight trip. Assign as many men as you see fit, as long as they're discreet."

"Where are you headed?"

"Greece."

"Ah." He barely hesitated for a moment. "I'll have the chopper ready to go inside of an hour. Please wait in your rooms until I come for you."

Considering he'd probably just given the giant of a man a heart attack, waiting to be fetched was the least Theo could do. "Of course. We'll be packed and ready." He hung up and turned to face Meg. She opened her mouth, but he got there first. "You can yell at me for the next few hours once we get on the transport."

"You can't just decide to leave like that."

Being in love with a cranky bastard like Galen had given Theo a lifetime of patience when dealing with a snarling significant other, but he still wanted to toss Meg over his shoulder and haul her ass to the helicopter to avoid continuing this argument. He gave her a long look, and she skittered back a step as if she could read his mind. "Don't you dare."

"You're right. We need to discuss the developments of the last few days, and we can't do it here." They couldn't do *anything* here in the palace. Not while the full list of their enemies remained shrouded in mystery. Not when everywhere Meg looked, she saw a reminder of what she perceived as their inequality. He'd suspected it grated on her, but he'd underestimated the strength of that irritation. No, better to go back to the last place all three of them had stood on equal footing and decide their path forward.

Together.

She opened her mouth, seemed to reconsider, and shut it. "You said Greece. You mean Galen's place?"

"Yes."

Finally, she nodded. "I'll pack."

"It's just overnight, princess. It's all I can promise." It would have to be enough. If they could just get through this...

There would be another crisis on the other side.

There would *always* be another crisis. Another issue. Another shit storm they had to buckle down and ride through.

If he was simply a noble, he could all but guarantee years of smooth sailing and relatively peaceful happiness. But Theo wasn't simply a noble. He was the fucking King of Thalania, and there would never be anything simple about his life.

Six months ago, both Galen and Meg had claimed to understand and work through the future together. Now, he wasn't sure when they'd been in more danger of drifting apart. No, drifting was too tame a word. Torn, shredded, cut to pieces.

If they couldn't find common ground in Greece, Theo didn't know that there was anything left for them to stand on.

DORIAN STORMED into his home and tossed his phone, sending it skittering over the marble countertops of the kitchen. "That fool!"

Anne barely looked up from her computer. "What did Huxley do this time?" It was a testament to their haphazard movement forward with the idiot Head of Huxley Family that she didn't feel the need to question who'd given him such a rage.

"He saw fit to inform our son that his whore of a daughter would happily jump into the bed vacated by Meg Sanders without the slightest hesitation."

Anne finally turned away from her computer and gave him her full attention. "It's a mistake to underestimate Noemi Huxley, Dorian. You may be able to dupe her father, but she's cut from a different cloth."

"That remains to be seen." She was ambitious—all nobles were ambitious—but she was too busy dallying with the help to strive for the kind of greatness a woman with her charm, looks, and intelligence could achieve. He couldn't have cast her better if he'd conjured her up himself.

All of it would be for naught if Galen rooted out their plan before it reached fruition. "Something needs to be done."

"Something was done." She picked up her wine glass and considered the merlot. "Ultimately nothing changes. Theodore already had his suspicions we were involved or he wouldn't have made a special trip out here just to subtly threaten you. We expected and planned for that eventuality."

Yes, they had. It didn't make this easier to stomach. "Huxley—"

"Has his own part to play. You knew this was a risk when you invited him to sit at the table."

He had. Of course he had. Dorian closed his eyes and took a deep breath. "I don't deserve you, my love."

"On that, I think we can both agree."

He laughed softly and gave himself a little shake. This was a minor setback, but ultimately all it did was change the timeline a bit. They were prepared. They'd *been* prepared since Theodore was exiled in the first place, knowing that their steps would leave them here. There was always the slightest possibility that the palace coup orchestrated by Philip Fitzcharles would work, but Dorian knew all too well how thoroughly Theodore's father had trained him. He wouldn't give up without a fight then, and he wouldn't now, either.

They simply had to give him an enemy to vanquish, a love to mourn, and then sweep in with their chosen candidate to reap the rewards.

Then, finally, they could stop circling on the fringes and step into the light where they belonged, their boots on the necks of their enemies and no one rising up to endanger them ever again.

Not a second too soon.

10

Meg didn't want to admit that Theo was right. She'd bottled up things for far too long, and all she wanted to do was yell and burn the entire situation to the ground. Healthy? No. Of course not. But there was no convenient guidebook for being in a relationship with two pigheaded men, both of whom occupied two of the highest positions of power in a freaking European country. Even if there *was*, she doubted she'd find a chapter titled, *Three Tips to Deal With The Fact Your New Friend Might Want to Kill and Replace You.*

Her feet had lost contact with solid ground weeks ago —*months* ago—and she was one wrong step away from a total free fall. Maybe it would be better...

No. She couldn't afford to think like that.

The helicopter touched down on the landing pad outside Galen's house and something in Meg's chest unclenched. This place held happy memories for her, despite everything. The last time they'd been there, they were on the run and Theo was facing down the truth that he might regain his throne, but he'd lose them in the process.

This was where she'd first met Isaac Kozlov, though he'd scared the shit out of her at the time. The place where she finally admitted that she loved Theo and Galen.

Night had long since fallen, and the view she knew was there on the opposite side of the property—the Aegean Sea —was barely more than a glint of moonlight on water here and there. Lights from the nearby towns created a haze along the coastline, but the water itself, her favorite part of this place, gave the illusion of hiding.

More apt than I want to admit.

"Meg."

Slowly, reluctance hindering her every move, she turned and followed Galen into the house. It looked identical to the first time she'd walked through the door, the upside-down U-shape housing the living room and kitchen on one end and the bedroom on the other. The entire back of the house was windows overlooking the infinity pool and the sea. Picturesque. Perfect.

Meg couldn't help looking at the stairs of the pool, couldn't stop the memories from rolling over her in a delicious wave. Galen on the steps. His cock in her mouth. Theo charging into the pool and fucking her against Galen's chest as if he could merge the three of them into one. Her breath hitched. She'd been so sure back then, so confident that she knew the right call, the right choice, the right path forward.

Now, she didn't know anything at all.

Meg slipped through the sliding glass door and kicked her shoes off to walk across the cool stone to the railing. Even with the house behind her, the darkness felt more absolute here. Stars winked overhead, and if she didn't know it was there, she'd have no idea that the other side of the patio railing fell away in a dizzying drop that would smash an unwary woman to pieces at the bottom. She inhaled deeply, letting the salty air roll through her. A few more deep breaths and she was as ready as she'd ever be to face the two men waiting for her inside.

By the time she walked back through the door, the security team was nowhere in sight. They weren't alone. They were never truly alone anymore. But at least they had the illusion of privacy.

Theo had pulled out a bottle of whiskey, and he lined up three shot glasses in front of him. When Meg had met him, she'd marveled that he handled himself around liquor like a veteran bartender. Now, she knew his skill stemmed from his father believing that deals were made over drinks, and if one was going to do something, they should learn to do it properly.

Theo poured shots into the three glasses and slid one over to her, and the middle one to Galen where he leaned against the kitchen counter. *He* hadn't said a single word since hearing that plans and changed and Greece was in their future. Meg picked up her glass and waited for the men to do the same, and all three took their shots as one.

She welcomed the burning down her throat, the way the whiskey warmed her stomach, the giddiness that shot through her. It faded almost immediately, but it felt good while it lasted. "Now what?"

Theo studied his empty glass. "In just under forty-eight hours, every Head of Family will descend on the palace."

"What? Why?"

"Because I invited them." He set the glass onto the counter with a soft clink. "We know Dorian is involved in the attack against you, but I can't be sure how deep the rot goes. Huxley is involved."

Meg rocked back on her heels. "Noemi didn't push me." When both men stared at her, she glared. "That's where you're going with this, isn't it? You think Noemi is dancing to the tune her father set and trying to scare me off."

"Kill you. Not scare you. Not drive you out of the country. Fucking murder you." Galen said. "They want you dead and gone."

She knew that, even if she hadn't been willing to state it aloud. There was something so fucked about near-strangers wanting her dead solely because of who she was fucking. No, not fucking. In love with. Love was so much more dangerous than sex, and anyone with half a brain knew that. Love made people do crazy things, like position someone with no qualifications and no lineage to speak of as Consort to an entire country.

"Not Noemi." Meg couldn't be sure of so many things in the current situation, but she was sure of that. She finally had a good read on the woman, she knew without a shadow of a doubt that Noemi was honest when she said she didn't want anything to do with the Consort position. "She's got her eye on a different prize."

"Whether or not she's in league with her father is irrelevant." Theo lined up the three glasses and poured another trio of shots. "Noemi is loyal to her Family and will continue to be so when all the chips have fallen. If that puts her on the other side of the line from us, she won't hesitate or let something as mundane as friendship stand in her way."

"I'm aware." She considered telling them both that Noemi could actually be a likely ally, but neither of her men seemed all that interested in hearing what she had to say. Not with Galen glowering like he wanted nothing more than to punch a hole through the wall, or Theo wearing his perfect politician expression.

It made Meg want to scream.

It wouldn't solve anything. She'd yell, Galen would snap

something jerky, and then Theo would be in the middle of it, and they'd accomplish nothing in the process. Meg didn't know the answer. It sure sounded like they had enemies in all directions and couldn't trust anyone but each other. She took a deep breath and strove for something resembling calm. "What are we going to do?" She looked from Theo to Galen and back again. "You said the Families are coming to the palace. What happens then?"

Galen took his shot and laughed hoarsely. "Then the bastard is going to offer you as bait, baby."

She waited for Theo to contradict him, to cut in and say he would never put her in that position. It didn't happen. He just met her gaze steadily, as unrepentant as ever. "It's the only way."

God, she could just throttle him. "And you didn't think that you might want to bring that to my attention sometime in the near future? Or, I don't know, maybe give me some warning *before* you put your brilliant plan into action."

"You can't act worth a damn, princess. I needed you to react naturally, and this was the only way."

Against all reason, her throat tried to close in on itself. He didn't trust her to be able to hold up her part of the plot. He just flat out didn't trust her. Good enough to fuck, but nowhere near good enough to be a full partner. The worst part in some ways was that any response she gave would only confirm his suspicions. If she screamed or cried or launched her shot glass at his head, his asshole assumptions would be proven correct and he'd *never* trust her.

Meg forced her spine straight and met his blue, blue eyes. It took everything she had to keep the quiver out of her voice. "In that case, I'm going swimming while the adults talk. Since I can't be trusted to handle myself." She turned and strode away.

He didn't call her back.

Had she really expected that he would? Meg prided herself on reading people. She always had. Too bad she'd missed the mark so badly with this situation. Her skin prickled, too tight, too angry, too much. Meg yanked her shirt off and kicked out of her pants. It was cold, but the steam rising off the pool told her that the water, at least, would be warm. After the slightest hesitation, she stripped out of her underwear as well. She waded into the pool and slipped beneath the surface.

The water closed over her head, encasing her, buoying her even as she tried not to cry over something as silly as her hurt pride. Meg stayed under until the ache in her chest became a real thing and then she let herself rise to the surface and float there, staring up at the stars overhead. With the patio lights unlit and the pool all shadows beneath her, she could almost pretend she floated among the stars instead of being tethered to the earth.

She felt him before she heard him, his big body moving through the water toward her, a pull in her stomach as if she'd swallowed a magnet attuned to only two men in the entire world. Meg didn't look over, didn't tear her attention from the sky overhead. "I don't need to be coddled."

"I know." Theo's voice slid out of the dark like some kind of crossroads demon. Tempting her to turn away from her anger the same way he tempted her from her path every time she thought it stable beneath her feet. "I'm sorry, princess."

"Are you?" That wasn't fair. She was just as much to blame as anyone—or at least just as responsible for the current situation. With the title of Consort weighing so heavily, she'd let herself be shuffled around because that was easier. Simpler.

She hadn't realized how much of a mistake it was until today.

They floated for several long minutes, and though he didn't make a move to touch her, she could feel the weight of his body occupying space just out of reach. If she concentrated, Meg could actually hear the water licking at his skin. She closed her eyes and inhaled, cursing herself for responding even though she was mad at him. Her breasts ached for his mouth, the faint breeze teasing her wet nipples to hard points. If he'd only touch her...

But no. They couldn't fuck away this problem. If that was possible, they would have accomplished it long before now. "If you can't trust me to be a full partner... What am I doing here, Theo? What's even the point?"

When he spoke, he was closer. "I'm not good at this, Meg. That probably doesn't need to be said, but I've spent so long trying to keep the people I care about safe, to stay one step ahead of my enemies, to be smarter, more ruthless, more willing to do whatever it takes to protect what's mine. I don't know how to just turn it off."

"I never wanted you to turn it off. Just extend that little inner circle to include one more person. You never would have put something like this into motion with Galen at the center without giving him some kind of head's up beforehand."

His silence was all the confirmation she needed. Meg closed her eyes, but the burning in her throat only stoked hotter with each breath. She would not cry. Crying was worthless and would only prove that Theo had made the right call. If she couldn't have a conversation with him without devolving into an emotional wreck then maybe—

No. Fuck that.

Theo took a deep breath that seemed to reach across the shrinking distance between them. "You're right."

Any admission was a win at this point, but it didn't feel like one with his words sliding beneath her skin like the sharpest of blades. She pressed her lips together, tasting salt from the pool. Or maybe from the tears she couldn't quite keep inside.

And then Theo was there, his hand sliding against hers, a tentative touch that she should have pushed aside, but even as angry and heartsore as she was, the only people she wanted comfort from was him and Galen. She laced her fingers through his and then he was there, pulling her into his arms and holding her so tightly, she could barely draw breath. "I'm sorry, Meg. Fuck, I know I screwed this up. Give me a chance to fix it. Please."

"We can't keep going on like we have been."

"I know."

Did he? With Theo, she could never be sure. He had the nasty habit of thinking that he could mold the world to his wishes and to hell with the consequences. The fact that he was usually right only made the whole thing more challenging, because people didn't really change. He would always make power moves first and ask for permission later, just like Galen would always step in between danger and the people he cared about without a second thought.

Just like Meg would always strive for independence, would fight against becoming too entrenched, against needing anyone too much. The fear of turning out like her mother—of proving her mother right—drove her harder than anything else in this world, and she didn't know how to turn it off any more than Theo and Galen could turn off their respective personality traits.

"Maybe this was doomed from the start." She didn't

realize she had any intention of saying the damning words aloud until they emerged, fully formed.

Theo ran his hands up her back and laced his fingers through her hair, urging her face up to meet his. Even in the dark, his gaze held her immobile. "Do you really believe that?"

Here, in this moment, she could offer nothing but truth. "I don't know."

"This will pass, Meg. We'll win. Things will settle down into a new normal." He stroked his thumbs over her cheekbones. "The only thing that we have a chance at keeping consistent is our relationship. Let me make this right."

"It's not supposed to be this hard." A childish plea, and she knew it. Life was hard. Life had *always* been hard for Meg. Had she honestly thought that rule would shift simply because she was in a relationship with a prince-turned-king? She'd known better, and she'd still fallen for the Prince Charming trap that spelled happily ever after for his chosen princess.

There was a reason the curtain fell in fairy tales immediately after the wedding, before reality could set in and both prince and new princess could figure out that falling in love was the easy part. Everything that came after? That's where the real work started, where relationships were made and broken in the trenches. Throw in a third person's wants and needs and they faced impossible odds to actually make their relationship work.

"Everything worth having requires a price, princess. You know that better than anyone."

Yeah, she did, but that didn't stop Meg from wanting to scream her frustration to the heavens. "No more lies, Theo —by omission or otherwise. If we're really in this together, then you need to actually let me in."

"Okay."

Easy for him to promise now, when they were naked beneath the new moon and their enemies were back in Thalania. Theo had always been good with his words, but when push came to shove, he did what he thought was best and to hell with the consequences. "We both know that promise isn't worth the breath you used to make it."

Theo pressed an achingly soft kiss to her forehead and stepped back, releasing her. "All I care about is that you're alive at the end of this, Meg. That's it. I'll do whatever it takes to ensure that happens. We both will."

The truth lay there before her. If faced with the choice between keeping her alive or losing her, he'd cut out his own heart and burn their relationship to the ground to ensure Meg remained among the living. Galen would do the same.

Either she could accept it and try to carve a path forward for all three of them or...

Or what?

She could leave?

The thought had a hysterical laugh pinging through her chest. She couldn't walk away from them any more than they could change the way they faced down threats. "This is hopeless."

"It's only hopeless if you let it be." He held out his hand, crooking his fingers at her. "Come on, princess. Galen and I have some apologizing to do."

She blinked. "Apologizing? Really? Don't you think that ship has sailed?"

His grin was a flash of white teeth in the shadows. "It's never too late to apologize. Come on."

Curious despite herself, she slipped her hand into his and let him tow her to the stairs leading out of the pool.

Meg shivered as the wind kicked up and lashed at her wet body, but they didn't linger outside. Theo led her through the sliding glass door and around the corner to the bedroom. The only door in the house lay against the far wall, and she knew from their previous time within this place that it housed a decadent bathroom to rival the one in their private suite back at the palace.

Theo nudged her toward that door. "Shower. We'll be ready for you when you're done."

She took a single step and stopped as Galen walked around the corner with a coil of silk rope in his hands. Meg's heart kicked against her ribs. She knew what that rope meant. Usually the kinkiest they got was the men taking turns topping, but on special occasions, Theo liked to play with bondage. During one particularly memorable time— one of their first—he'd tied her up as punishment and fucked Galen in front of her. Her body tightened in response to that memory as much as she shivered in anticipation of what would come.

She ducked into the bathroom and took the quickest shower on record. Meg dried off and padded back into the bedroom. In the five minutes she'd been gone, they'd shifted the room around. A high-backed chair now occupied the space at the foot of the bed, and for the life of her she couldn't figure out where it had come from. The comforter and top sheets were gone, leaving only the fitted sheet covering the mattress, and two sets of padded cuffs lay attached to rope that appeared to have been looped beneath the mattress itself. They had to have been crazy long since the bed was so big, but it couldn't be clearer what the intent was.

"Punishment, Theo? Really?" She meant for the words to come out sarcastic, but they were too breathy.

"Not for you, princess." Theo moved to stand behind the chair and motioned for her to sit.

She shot a glance at Galen, but he had his unreadable expression on. She'd get nothing from him until this ran its course. Meg gave a theatrical sigh and walked to sit gingerly in the chair. A quick look around found no ropes to tie her with, which was a small relief. She absolutely loved Theo's punishments. The man could be downright devious when inspired, and he put that twisty mind of his to good use in their little sexual power games, but Meg wasn't in the mood to play the helpless third yet again. It normally turned her on so much, she could barely breathe past her need, but tonight it would ring a little too true.

Of course Theo knew that. He was too smart not to.

He sifted his fingers through her damp hair, moving it off her neck as he leaned around to press a kiss to her temple. "Tonight, you're in charge. Tell us what you want, and it's yours. Anything goes."

Her breath stilled in her lungs. "Anything?" Her mind tripped over itself to provide fantasy after fantasy. They'd worked through so many of her deepest desires in the time they'd been together, but nothing short of a lifetime would exhaust her need for them.

Galen gave a short nod. "Fucking anything."

Meg bit her bottom lip, striving for something resembling control. "I want you naked and on your knees."

Theo pressed on last kiss to her temple. "What our princess wants, our princess gets."

11

Fury drove Galen's need for penance as much as guilt. The things he cared about most in this world were unraveling around him and he couldn't do a single damn thing to stop it. If it was as simple as putting a bullet in his old man's head... Well, it wasn't as easy as that anymore. It hadn't been in a long time. Dorian's reach was too overarching, the tentacles of his influence dug too deep.

They might lose Meg over this, and it might not even be because he failed to protect her.

She sat in that chair like a fucking queen who deserved to be worshiped, and he had to clamp down hard on the insane desire to demand her forgiveness. She couldn't grant it over something he wasn't even fucking sorry about. He'd lie to her and worse to ensure she stayed safe. From the look in her hazel eyes, she knew it, too. She tilted her head to the side, so regal it made his chest ache. "Problem, Galen?"

"No." He pulled his shirt over his head and tossed it aside, quickly followed by his jeans. Beside him, Theo stood silently. He hadn't bothered to get dressed after chasing her down in the pool, and with his hair wet and slicked back he looked sharper, as if somewhere in the last hour he'd cut away a layer of civility he usually kept as close as a second skin.

They went to their knees as one, and fuck if it didn't feel right.

Meg never topped. Not really. She liked to run her mouth and push them, and occasionally that included a flare of a dominant side he liked to provoke when the mood suited him. But usually he or Theo took the reins and she was happily along for the ride.

Not tonight.

Tonight had tipped them over the edge into completely new territory, and he didn't know where they'd end up. The thought rankled. Galen liked to be ten steps ahead in any given situation, and he didn't know what tomorrow would bring, let alone further down the timeline.

It scared the shit out of him.

"You're thinking too hard, Galen." Meg taped a finger against her knee. "I don't think he's as committed to this as you are, Theo."

Theo shot him a warning look, the faintest flaring in his blue eyes. "Maybe you should give him some incentive."

"Maybe so." Meg took a short breath, as if bracing herself. "Come here, baby. I need your mouth on me." When Galen shifted, she pointed at him. "Not you. You can sit there and think about what you've done, and watch while Theo tongues my pussy." She gave him a mocking smile. "Or not watch, as the case may be. I doubt you'll get much of a show from that angle."

She was right.

Galen clenched his fists as Theo moved to kneel before Meg and spread her thighs wide. Sure enough, from his current position, he could only see the back of Theo's dark head as his best friend dipped down. Meg arched her spine and reached down to lace her fingers through Theo's hair. Her breath hitched the way it always did when one of them touched her, and Galen didn't have to see everything in explicit detail to know Theo had just dragged his tongue over her clit. A flush spread over her cheeks and down her chest as her eyes met his. She lifted her chin in challenge, daring him to break ranks even as her breathing picked up.

He forced his hands to relax and dragged his gaze over the lines of Theo's back, the bunch of his muscles under his skin as he gripped Meg's thighs with his hands and fucked her with his tongue.

I need to see.

"That's enough, Theo." Meg pushed him gently away from her and used her foot to urge him back. She considered them. "I am so mad at both of you."

It was hard to think with her naked and wet from Theo's mouth. Galen forced himself to meet her gaze. "Do you want an apology?"

"What would be the point?" She twisted a strand of her dark hair around a single finger. "Neither of you are actually sorry, and you'd both do the exact same thing again if given half the chance."

She wasn't wrong, but he'd never meant to cause her pain. Galen *protected*. It what he did. It was who he was. He didn't know how to balance that against the softness Meg needed sometimes. Theo was better at that shit, but he'd been so damn distracted lately, their whole triad had shifted out of balance.

"Tell us what you want, princess." Theo ran a hand through his hair, the movement nowhere near as carefree as it usually was. He shook, just a little, barely holding it together.

Neither of them took to submission naturally. The power games and fucking around with each other and Meg was never quite so defined as it stood in that moment. They needed her trust. They needed her forgiveness, even if neither of them deserved it. Theo practically shook with the strength of that need, and Galen instinctively reached out to press his hand to the center of his man's back. "Breathe. She's not leaving us."

"Isn't she?"

"*She* is sitting right here." But something in Meg's gaze softened. She crooked a finger at Theo. "Come here, baby."

He crawled to her, the King of Thalania willingly on his knees for one of the loves of his life. Galen had never seen a more unnatural thing in his life. Theo wasn't meant to be subservient to anyone—not even Galen. He stood above all others when he walked into a room, his presence announcing him as much as his position.

Meg urged him up on his knees in front of her, Theo's height putting them nearly even. She leaned forward and captured his chin. "I'm not leaving you. Either of you."

Theo shuddered out a nearly silent breath, but Galen heard it all the same. Meg stroked his bottom lip with her thumb. "But if you pull this shit again, I'm going to tie you up at the end of our bed the same way you did to me that first time, and I'm going to play with myself until your cock is so hard, you can't string together two words." She kissed him lightly. "And then I'm going to go fuck whichever one of you I'm less pissed at while the other watches. It will be torturous and maybe a little painful, and not at all fun. Do you understand?"

"Yeah."

She looked at Galen, clearly waiting for a response. He

snorted. "Baby, I like to watch. That doesn't sound like much of a punishment to me."

"You are so damn difficult. You like to watch, Galen? Then watch." She stood and motioned for Theo to take her place. He'd barely gotten seated before Meg straddled him and took his mouth. Theo gripped her hips, but she grabbed his hands and guided them to the arms of the chair. "No touching."

She rolled her body against Theo's, giving him one hell of a lap dance. He dug his fingers into the wood of the chair and clenched his jaw as Meg turned around to face Galen and wrapped her fist around Theo. "Such a lovely cock." She gave him a stroke. "So hard and needing what only we can provide. Who do you want to take care of you, Theo?"

"Is that a trick question?"

"Maybe." She laughed, the sound pulling at Galen despite his best efforts to play this game to the very end. "I'm so empty, baby. I need you to fill me up." She guided him into her and sank down in a single smooth stroke.

Both their faces went fucking blissful and despite himself, something like jealousy spiked through Galen. He wasn't the one who put all the fucked up plans into motion. Theo was. And yet Theo was buried to the hilt in Meg's sweet pussy, and Galen was left here, the cold floor digging into his bare knees and his cock so hard, he wasn't sure he had any blood left in his body.

Meg lifted her arms over her head, turning her body into one rolling line, drawing his gaze from her hands to her mouth to her tits and down to where Theo's cock disappeared into her pussy. She met his gaze and spread her legs wider, giving him more of a show. From this angle, he could see how wet Theo's cock was, how wet *she* was.

"Fuck."

He hadn't realized he'd spoken aloud until Meg grinned. "Got you." She cupped her breasts, an offering he couldn't accept unless she gave an explicit order. "Tell me, Galen. Is watching really better? Or do you want to be over here? Touching me?" She pinched her nipples and then stroked her hands down her stomach. "Your hands all over me?" She reached down and cupped Theo's balls. "Driving Theo out of his goddamn mind?"

Theo cursed. "I'm hanging on by a thread here, princess."

"Keep hanging on. You don't come until I say so." She gave him one last squeeze and released him. "Come here, Galen."

Galen's place wasn't normally on his knees, and crawling created an extension of that unnatural feeling, but hell if it didn't feel a whole lot like the apology he wasn't sure he planned on offering. Meg, somehow, knew exactly where his mind had gone. She shivered a little and cupped his face when he finally made it close enough to touch them. "You make me crazy."

"Feeling's mutual."

"Mmhmm." She released him and leaned back to brace herself on Theo's arms. "Make me come, baby." She guided Theo's hands to her hips. "Both of you."

Galen didn't need to be told twice. He leaned down and dragged his tongue over her as Theo drew her down hard on his cock. Meg made that cute little whimpering sound she did when she was in danger of losing it, and it drove Galen wild. He sucked her clit hard, setting his teeth against the sensitive bundle of nerves. Once. Twice. A third time. That was all it took. Meg's back bowed as she came, her cries loud enough to shake the room.

It wasn't enough.

Fuck it, but he *had* fucked up. If this was his penance, then so be it, but he'd damn well do it right. He lifted Meg off Theo's cock and slid her higher onto his chest so he had better access to her pussy. What little control he had left after watching her play with Theo snapped. He couldn't get enough of this woman—and this man—and he wasn't interested in trying. Meg might not be thinking of leaving now, but if they kept fucking up, she *would* eventually get tired of their shit and walk.

He wanted to chain her to them, to bind her with pleasure and need and love until she couldn't stand the thought of a life lived without them at her back. It wasn't a battle for tonight alone. No, it would take Galen days and weeks and months and fucking *years* to convince her to stay, to build up a strong enough foundation that nothing could rock them.

And he couldn't do it alone.

He looked up Meg's body and met Theo's gaze. Understanding flashed between them, as monumental as a lightning strike. They would start tonight. They would make things right, and they would wake in the morning as a whole unit, stronger for the shit they were about to walk through.

MEG HAD LOST CONTROL. She hadn't had a game plan going in to this, but if she had, it wouldn't involve Galen fucking her with his tongue, the frantic possessiveness of his mouth against her pussy already driving her toward another orgasm. She reached back, and Theo caught her hands, pinning them easily on either side of his head. He buried his face against the side of her neck, kissing and nipping, something akin to desperation in every touch. He shifted his grip so he held both her wrists in one hand and cupped one of her breasts with the other. "I'll never get enough of you."

She could fight this, could reassert herself into the game he'd laid out at the start...

Meg didn't want to.

She didn't want penance. She wanted their version of normal, for the balance to be restored, for them to reclaim *them*.

Letting go was the only way. She shivered under Galen's mouth. "Don't stop." He didn't. He kept up his thorough tongue fucking, driving her closer and closer to the edge.

"Do you feel how much he loves you, princess? How much he needs you?" Theo's voice curled around her, more seductive than any devil. "He'd be lost without you. We both would."

Galen sucked on her clit hard, just the way she liked it, and she lost her breath as an orgasm rolled through her. Her brain shorted out and her body went limp. She lolled her head to Theo's for a kiss, and then Galen was there, dragging his mouth along her neck on the other side.

She never felt safer than when pinned between these two men.

She needed more, for them to overwhelm her and banish the last of the bad feelings that had lingered over the last few days, growing stronger with each realization that they had shut her out. *Never again. I won't allow it.* "More. I need more."

"Greedy little thing, aren't you?" Galen murmured against her skin.

She grabbed the back of his neck. "You're as angry at him as I was."

Galen hesitated for the barest hint of a second. "Yeah, I am."

"We purge it all tonight. All the bad stuff. We work it out on each other."

Behind her, Theo had gone still. "It's not that easy."

"It's as easy as we make it." There would be time for conversations and bickering and plotting in the morning. Tonight was theirs and theirs alone. She nudged Galen back and climbed to her feet. Her legs wobbled a little, but they held her. Meg padded to the bed and climbed onto the tall mattress, all too aware of both their attention on her. She turned and sat on the edge of it. They stood there, her two men, so alike and so different at the same time. They loved her. She never doubted that for a second. It was just all the other bullshit that got in the way.

"What do you need, princess?"

She licked her lips, need already coiling through her again. "I want you to fuck me. I need to lose myself in you."

The men exchanged a look and then Theo stepped forward. He kissed her and pressed her back into the mattress, his hand delving between their bodies to push a finger and then two inside her. As if his cock hadn't spent part of tonight already buried inside her. But that was Theo, careful to the very end. Meg grabbed his wrist and brought his hand up so she could suck his two fingers into her mouth. She gave them both a long lick and sat back. "I don't want you to be careful with me tonight. I want all of you."

She wanted him there with them, just as raw and open and honest as Theo always required of them. He loved to dig in deep and pick them apart at the seams, but he held himself back even when in the midst of the most intimidate lovemaking Meg had ever experienced. She could count on one hand how many times she'd seen him lose control and still have fingers left over. Tonight, he hovered on the edge. There was something dangerous in his blue eyes, and she wanted to light the match that would send it up in flames.

Galen knew. Galen always knew where she was headed. They were too similar for it to be any other way. He crawled onto the bed behind her and pulled her away from Theo's touch, only stopping when they were out of reach. "You've gone too easy on him, baby."

She leaned against him, his solid presence at her back making her heart beat harder. "You want to punish him."

"Fuck yes, I do." He pointed at Theo. "You want to apologize. What just happened was barely a start. Stand right fucking there and don't move until we give you permission."

Theo looked from one of them to the other. He finally nodded, the movement jerky with pent up emotion. "So be it."

"You need it rough, baby." Galen carefully bracketed her throat and bent her body against his, bowing her back and putting her on display. "You want me to pound that pussy while Theo drives himself crazy wishing it was his cock buried inside you, feeling you clench around him like a fucking fist, knowing how wet he's got you?"

She couldn't see Theo's face from her position, but she didn't need to. His soft curse as Galen dragged a finger over her was truth enough. Meg shivered and rolled her hips, inviting Galen in. "Yes."

"Mmm." His finger continued its path south, circling lower. "Or I'll fuck your tight little ass while he watches, knowing your pussy is waiting for him, *aching* for him, and he's not allowed to touch."

Oh god.

She wanted it. She wanted it all.

Meg swallowed hard, the move pressing her throat more firmly against Galen's palm. "Or maybe you should flip me over and fuck me while he fantasizes about fucking *your* ass while you're inside me."

Galen's hand spasmed and he pushed two fingers into her pussy, cupping her there possessively. She didn't need to look to know he was watching Theo as he finger fucked her. "She knows what you like."

"Of course she does." Theo's voice barely sounded like his own. "She's ours. How could she not?"

12

———

Theo gripped the edge of the mattress as if that would be enough to root him in place as he watched Galen run his hands over Meg, his furious filthy words coloring the room around them. Taunting. Searching for just the right trigger. Any other time, Theo would have fought for control, assuming it as naturally as breathing. When push came to shove, both Galen and Meg deferred to him. They loved it too much not to.

But he owed them an apology, and if he could barely force the words past his lips, he could damn well hang on long enough to suffer through their punishment.

He'd certainly delivered enough of his own over the last six months, for infractions both real and imagined. His Meg liked to play games, and he enjoyed filling that need for her.

She wasn't his in that moment, though.

She was Galen's, well and truly.

Galen had her caged with his body, one hand bracketing her throat, and the other gripping her pussy possessively. The challenge in his lover's dark eyes didn't need to be spoken to be understood. *Mine.*

Not fucking likely.

They didn't compete over her. They were each other's as much as they were hers, as much as she was theirs. The power dynamic might shift a little from time to time to adapt as necessary, but despite Meg's fears, it *was* mostly equal.

Not tonight.

Tonight, for the first time in six months, Theo stared down the barrel at what his future might have been if Galen and Meg weren't too stubborn by half. Him, standing alone, an untouchable pillar forever destined to be separate from those around him. Them, very much of the earth, very much each other's. Galen, owning Meg, being owned by Meg.

Without him.

Galen, damn him to hell and back, was proving a point. He toppled Meg onto her back, with her head near the end of the bed where Theo stood. "Arms over your head, baby. Give him a show." He spread her legs wide and guided his big cock into her. One hand went back to her throat in ownership and he drove into her hard enough to send her several inches up the mattress. He managed to keep himself off her body enough to give Theo a show that had him clenching his jaw so hard it was a wonder his teeth remained intact.

They were so fucking beautiful together, Galen all brutal power and scars, and Meg feminine curves and tangled dark hair. His Beauty and his Beast. His... Unless he lost them.

Theo hit his knees next to the mattress, unable to tear his gaze from where Galen's cock disappeared into her. "I'm sorry. I'm so fucking sorry."

"Mmm." Galen slowed his pace, teasing Theo as much as he teased Meg. "That's a start."

"Sadist," Meg whispered, a thread of amusement winding through the desire in her voice. "You want him to beg."

"Don't you?"

She tilted her head back and met Theo's eyes. Even half gone with pleasure, Meg seemed to see down to the very heart of him. She reached up and grabbed his wrists, anchoring him in place. "I have his apology. I want his cock."

"You're too easy on him, baby. You make a terrible top." Galen stopped moving, buried inside her to the hilt. He smoothed his hand down the center of her body and back up again. For a moment, it looked like his perverse need to be an ass would get the best of him, but he finally shook his head. "You're in charge."

"Glad someone remembered it." She inched closer to the edge of the mattress, and Galen moved with her, keeping them sealed together. She gave Theo's wrists a squeeze. "Come here."

He obeyed, slightly shocked to find his legs weren't quite steady. Meg fisted his cock, a slow smile pulling at the edges of her lips. "Do you know what I want, Theo?"

"Tell me." He'd assume nothing. Not tonight. Not with them. Not anymore.

"I want you to fuck my mouth while Galen fucks my pussy."

Galen spoke filth all the time. It was something that Theo loved and expected from him. Every time Meg did it, though? He lost his fucking mind. There was something about the crude words falling from those angel lips that drew him in a way he was never full prepared for. Even after all this time.

Meg tilted her head half off the mattress, leaving her throat in a single long line. An invitation Theo couldn't resist even if he was so inclined. He leaned over the bed and let her guide his cock between her lips, licking him with the same sinful tongue that had just spilled words that made his body clench with need. She sucked him deep once, and then again, and on the third time, she set her teeth against his sensitive base. A reminder of her command.

Theo lifted his gaze to meet Galen's, seeing the same storm of emotions in the other man's eyes that swirled through his chest. They didn't deserve her. Times like these only drove that reality home. No other woman in all their history together had seen to the very heart of them and strove to give them what they needed, even if they couldn't admit it themselves.

There was no other woman they'd trusted enough to allow into their very hearts.

He pulled almost all the way out of her mouth and then thrust carefully back in, testing her. Meg had taken mouth fuckings before, but easing into it was the only way to ensure everyone had a good time, no matter what she demanded. He went to withdraw again, but she grabbed his thighs and dug her nails in.

A silent command for *more*.

"Damn it, princess, I'm trying not to hurt you."

"She's ours, you idiot. Trust her." Galen lifted her hips and drove into her, his grip holding her in place so he didn't shove her deeper onto Theo's cock as he fucked her.

It had never been a problem before. But then, Theo had never been in his own head quite the same way he was tonight. He hesitated, torn between what he wanted to do and what he knew he should do.

Meg pushed him away and cursed. "Galen, this isn't working. He's thinking too much."

Galen pulled out of her and sat back on his heels. Theo

knew him well enough for warning bells to be pealing at the sight of those dark eyes going darker with cunning. "On the bed. Now."

~

INSPIRATION STRUCK as Meg watched Theo climb up to join them on the mattress. She grabbed Galen's hand. "Hold on." Both men froze, waiting for her command. The sheer power rush of having these two obeying her, even if it was only for tonight, left her giddy. "Theo, baby, do you remember that fight we had back in New York?"

He frowned, dark brows lowering. "You'll have to be more specific."

"You had me on the kitchen counter and you were licking my pussy and telling me how much you missed me." Her body tightened in response to the memory as much as a reaction to their proximity. She sat up and ran a hand down each of their chests. Galen's dusky skin had pale scars criss-crossing it, seemingly at random, but Theo's paler skin was mostly untouched. So different and yet so similar at the same time. She shivered. "You were telling me what you'd been fantasizing about while you fucked Galen."

His frown cleared and his eyes turned to searing blue flames. "Fucking him while he fucked you."

"Yes." A first for them. They'd had each other in so many ways, in all different combinations and positions. Never like this. She didn't know why they'd held off, but it ended tonight. "That's what I want." She twisted to look around, her gaze settling on the large windows. With a little light in the bedroom, they'd turn into mirrors. Meg crawled around them to the nightstand and flicked on the lamp. *Yes, like that.*

She climbed to her feet and shot them a look. "What are you waiting for?"

Galen moved before she'd finished speaking. He circled the mattress and looped an arm around her hips, dropping her onto her back on the bed. "Look at the window, baby. That's what you wanted, isn't it?"

She watched the reflection of him spread her legs wider, watched his big body tower over her prone one, and nearly moaned from the sight alone. "Yes. This is what I want."

"You heard her, Theo." Galen braced his hand on the bed beside her neck and slipped his other between her thighs, fingering her pussy. One stroke deep inside her, one stroke dragging over her clit, alternating until her hips moved of their own volition, writhing to take him deeper.

Her gaze went to Theo, still sitting on the edge of the mattress, watching them. She'd never seen him look so tormented, and it made her want to wrap him up with the only comfort he'd allow himself. It wasn't an option right now. He wouldn't take her forgiveness, her soft comfort, but he'd take *this*.

He'd take them.

Finally Theo moved, first to the nightstand to grab the lube Galen kept stashed there and then to the foot of the bed. Meg watched him in the reflection, watched the stiff movements go fluid as Galen guided his cock inside her. It felt so damn good to be filled like this, to be here with them both, to be just one part of a whole. Meg spent so much time fighting for her independence that she never would have expected to find this kind of peace in the act of losing herself.

She knew the exact moment Theo pushed into Galen. It was there in the tension of the bigger man's body, the way he went still inside *her* and blew out a slow breath. There was no time to adjust to any of it. It was as if entering Galen broke something in Theo. He pushed the other man down on top of her and grabbed her wrists to pin them at the back of Galen's neck. Only Galen's bracing on his elbows keeping their full weight off Meg's body. The move shoved Galen's cock even deeper into her, and she buried her face in his neck, gasping and whimpering and making noises she had no name for.

"This is what you wanted." Each of Theo's words accompanied a savage thrust into Galen, rocking him deeper into her. "You want me off the leash? I'm off the fucking leash, princess."

Meg turned her head just enough to watch them in the mirror. It was the only movement she was capable of, pinned as she was with legs splayed and her hands trapped. The sight of them... It stole her what little breath she had left. Theo was all brutal power as he drove into Galen, and for once the tension had bled out of Galen's muscles, his body moving in time with Theo's, pushing back against each thrust. Sweat slicked all their skin, leaving them shining a little in the low light, all askew limbs and shared breaths and rough sliding motion.

This. This is what we need.

To each be part of their whole. To be reminded of what they'd sacrificed so much for.

Her orgasm caught her unawares. One moment she was clinging to Galen and luxuriating in the steadily building pleasure spiraling through her, and the next her body clenched down hard and everything went fuzzy as she cried out. It set off a chain reaction, Galen cursing and thrusting hard into her again and again, driving himself into her and driving Theo harder into him. He laced his fingers through hers so he could brace himself to get a better angle and then he was coming in great spurts she swore she could actually feel inside her. He slumped down half on top of her.

But Theo wasn't done.

He pulled out of Galen and stared down at them. "Don't move."

As if they were capable of it at this point. She watched Theo stalk to the bathroom and heard the shower start, but Meg couldn't do more than nudge Galen off her so she could draw a full breath. "We're in trouble."

"Yeah." He didn't bother to lift his head.

Good. They'd woken a piece of Theo he purposefully kept hidden, and Meg couldn't bring herself to regret it. Whatever else the night brought, it'd demolished the walls they'd spent six long months building between each other. Or at least it'd started the process.

Theo walked out of the bathroom a few minutes later smelling of the woodsy soap Galen kept the place stocked with. He pushed Galen's thigh off Meg's legs and spread her wide. She bit her bottom lip as he pushed a single finger into her. "He filled you up, didn't he, princess?"

"Yes," she breathed. It felt so wrong to talk like that, to have Theo looking at her pussy filled with Galen's cum with the kind of possessiveness that, in another time in her life, would have sent her sprinting from the room. He looked at her like she was his pet, a favored toy to play with, and his favorite flavor, all rolled into one.

He notched his cock at her entrance and slid into her in a single move. The frenzy had gone from his movements, but there was something in his blue eyes that she didn't have a name for. Something that turned her on as much as it spooked her. Theo cupped her breasts with rough hands, stroked down her sides, and squeezed her hips.

Knowing her. Claiming her. Marking her.

"One day, princess." He covered her with his body and laced his fingers through hers the same way Galen had a when he came. Theo dipped down and sucked hard on her neck. "One day, when you're ready, this will be how it starts. Galen will fill you up, and then I'll fuck you until we're so mixed inside you, there's no telling where he ends and I begin. Until it's just *us*." He licked the shell of her ear.

Her mind tried to connect the dots even as she shied away from what he was saying. Meg writhed, unsure if she wanted him closer or to push him away. Galen's muttered curse only deepened her confusion. "What?"

"You know what." Another thrust. Another hard suction against her neck. "Someday you're going to have our baby, princess."

"Holy shit." She couldn't move, couldn't think, couldn't do *anything*. She twisted enough to look at Galen, trying to ignore the way she instinctively wrapped her legs around Theo's waist to keep him deep inside her. Her mind might be scrambling to catch up, but her body was already down with every word spilling out of Theo's mouth. "Is that what you want?"

Galen traced her face with his gaze and then looked at Theo. He tried to throw up his usual indifference, but something raw peered through. *Need*. Need that took her breath away. He let her look her fill, and then he turned away. "When you're ready."

"What if I'm never ready?" The words popped out before she had a chance to reconsider. She didn't even know if she *wanted* to reconsider. In all the conversations they'd had, somehow kids had never come up. Looking back, she had to admit that there was likely a reason for that. They'd intentionally left the conversation for—

Theo gave a short pump that took her breath away. She

moaned. "You two are such assholes for throwing stuff like that as me when I've got one of your cocks buried deep and I'm so close to coming I can't see straight."

Theo pressed another of those long, slow kisses against her neck, setting his teeth against her sensitive skin. "If you're never ready, then you're never ready."

As if it was as simple as that.

Maybe, for him, it was.

Meg arched up and kissed him. She didn't want to talk about babies or the future or what tomorrow would bring. She just wanted *this* for as much time as they could carve out. Tomorrow would come soon enough.

Tonight. They had tonight.

THEO WOKE before the other two and put together a particularly strong pot of coffee. He watched the dark liquid drip into the pot and smiled despite everything. Last night had been... cathartic. It might not have rocked the rest of the world from its axis, but Galen and Meg never failed to rock *his* world. Last night, they'd taken the first step toward fixing what he'd nearly broken in his stubbornness.

Even now, Theo wasn't sure he'd made the wrong choice.

"You weren't planning on ditching us and running back to Thalania to face down our enemies alone, were you?"

Theo turned and leaned against the counter. Meg had pulled on one of Galen's shirts, and the fabric dwarfed her. With her dark hair a wild tangle around her face and shoulders and red marks from their mouths all over her thighs, she looked so fucking tempting, he almost went to her right then and there.

Almost.

But he'd made a promise, and fucking until they couldn't stand wasn't part of the equation. The sun had risen, and with it their responsibilities. Their path forward.

He pulled two mugs down from the cabinet. "The thought did cross my mind."

"Remember what happened last time you tried to send us off to safety while you faced down the dragons? It didn't work then, and it won't work now."

"I'm beginning to see that." He poured coffee into both the mugs and passed one over to her. "I *am* sorry, princess. I want you two safe. That's it."

Meg gave him a sad smile. "That's not it, Theo. It might be in the top three, but you want your country to flourish. You want your people to be safe and thriving. You want to be king. You want a lot of things beyond just safety. You could have had safety in New York, and it wasn't enough."

The words cut right to the heart of him. Theo actually pressed a hand to his chest, half expecting to find she'd drawn blood. "You really think you're not enough for me?"

"No one is enough for you." She held up a hand. "That came out wrong. You weren't destined for a simple life, and I knew that when I signed on. So did Galen. Trying to keep us separate from everything else—trying to keep *me* separate— is a mistake. The only way this works is if we merge everything together. You have to realize that."

Even now, even with so much at stake, he resisted the idea. "You have given up everything to be here with us. Asking for more—"

"Wow, Theo, god complex much?" Meg picked up her mug and cradled it between her palms. "I made my choices, and I own them. Yeah, I let myself get swept up in the bullshit, and that's my bad, and I definitely need to establish some boundaries with Alys. You didn't club me over the head and haul me home to your palace as your captive. I chased you down. Share the burden, okay?"

Easier said than done. All his life, he'd been painfully aware of the responsibility that came with his birthright. Being king was a heavy weight to bear. His father had taken it seriously and wanted Theo to do the same, so his training had started when he was still too young to fully understand what would be required of him. He'd had thirty-odd years to come to terms with his role and what it required. Meg had had two weeks. Was it any wonder she'd faltered in the last six months?

"I wasn't as there for you as I should have been."

"No, you weren't." She shrugged. "But I didn't ask for help, either."

If Meg and Galen were two halves to the same whole, he'd never stopped to consider the things she and *Theo* had in common and how it would alter their relationship as time went on. For better or worse, they were both prideful creatures that let the need not to lean on anyone around them drive them to ridiculous lengths.

He walked to her and waited for her to set the mug down so he could pull her into his arms. Theo rested his chin on the top of her head and inhaled deeply. "We need to check in more regularly."

"Probably."

"Definitely." He held her close and let her steady heartbeat reassure him. "There is no convenient guidebook for this sort of thing."

"If there was, you wouldn't read it anyways." She laughed softly. "Since when do you take any direction but your own?"

"I'm a work in progress." It was even the truth. He'd been

the captain of a sinking ship, frantically patching holes to keep it afloat, rather than asking for assistance from the crew standing by. "I'll learn to delegate if you promise to tell me when you're feeling overwhelmed."

Galen walked into the room and snorted. "And maybe pigs will fly."

Meg turned in Theo's arms, and he didn't need to see her expression to know she was glaring at Galen. "I'm capable of asking for help."

"Since when?" He crossed his arms over his chest and stared her down. "Was it when you realized it was a smart ass choice to talk to *us* instead of going to Noemi fucking Huxley for help? Or maybe it was all those times in the last few months when you admitted you were drowning and reached out?" He raised his eyebrows. "My memory must be faulty because I don't remember any of that shit happening."

"Galen," Theo sank a world of warning into the name.

"No, fuck you with that shit. I'll get to you in a minute." He didn't tear his gaze from Meg's face. "You're pissed that we moved on this without you? *You* shut us out first. You started shutting us out the first time you fucked up at the Consorts' dinner, and you've spent the last six months wedging the door between us farther closed. So don't fucking play the victim here, Meg. *You* made the choice, same as we did. It was the wrong choice all around, but you were equal partner in getting us to this point, so you're damn well going to be equal partner in getting us out of it."

Meg seemed to wilt in his arms, but he actually felt the moment she decided to step to the line Galen had drawn in the sand. Her spine went to steel and she shrugged out of Theo's embrace. "Fine. I'll admit that I need help when *you* admit you hate being Consort and want your old job as head of security back."

Theo rocked back on his heels. "What?" He'd known Galen was grappling with the role of Consort, same as Meg, but he hadn't realized...

He hadn't realized a lot, apparently.

Meg wasn't finished, though. She closed the distance between her and Galen and poked him in the chest. "Did *you* tell Theo that you were miserable? Did you try to find a solution? No need to answer. I know for a fact you didn't, either. So reconsider throwing stones from that glass house of yours."

Galen opened his mouth, but Theo got there first. "That's enough." He stepped around Meg and positioned himself between them. "If you wanted to be head of security again, why didn't you just say something?"

"I'm Consort."

Theo stared, waiting for more, but Galen didn't seem interested in elaborating. Finally, Theo sighed. "Yes, you are. And?"

"And... I'm Consort. Consort has a specific set of duties. That's how things work."

If he didn't love the man so much, he might actually throttle him. Theo ran his hands over his face. "Galen, we're already breaking a couple centuries' worth of tradition by having a royal triad with two Consorts. What is the fucking point of doing this if we're all so miserable that we're at each other's throats?" He held up a hand before either of them could jump in. "This being king and Consorts, not this being our relationship."

Galen finally *looked* at him. "You're serious."

"Of course I'm fucking serious. I didn't name you Consort so I could cram the two of you into pre-existing molds. We already broke the damn molds just by existing in public like we do." He gripped Galen's shoulders. "Do you want to be head of security again?"

Galen looked away and back, a muscle twitching in his jaw. "Yes."

"Fuck, was that so hard? We'll make it happen."

He shook his head. "After. After we get through this."

He had a point. Theo nodded. "Then it's time to talk about what that will take."

Galen shrugged out from beneath his hands. "Not yet." He moved until he stood nearly shoulder to shoulder with Meg. "You haven't grieved for your old man, Theo. You haven't dealt with any of the emotional shit that comes from being back in this place. You think charging forward and dragging us along behind you will solve everything and it fucking won't."

He might as well have punched Theo in the face. He took a step back, feeling as if they had him on the ropes. "That's not fair."

"It's truth." This from Meg. She spoke with half the volume, but her words hit just as hard. "How are we supposed to bare everything when you are keeping important stuff locked away? It's okay to grieve, Theo. You loved him and he's gone and then you were hit with exile immediately after. It's okay to slow down long enough to feel something, even if it hurts."

Pressure clamped around his chest, a grinding terrible thing that stole his breath and snapped the ties on his control. "I'll grieve my father when and how I choose to."

"Fine." Galen's glare intensified. "As long as you do it. Stop bottling that shit up, Theo. You're going to explode and you're going to take all of us down when you do."

Meg elbowed him. "What Galen is trying—and failing—

to say is that we want you to be happy and we know this is hurting you. Maybe talking about it will help."

What would talking do? His father was gone, and he'd never really know if his death was caused by poison or nature taking its course. Exhuming the body was out of the question. His position was already precarious enough without someone taking those actions as ones a madman would put into play and using it against Theo. They had already broken tradition in so many ways—the exile, the triad, the number of foreigners in vital positions within the palace. Adding another to the list might be the tipping point they didn't come back from.

Maybe they *shouldn't* come back from it.

"What if we just left?"

Meg looked at him as if he was speaking in tongues. "What are you talking about?"

"What if we left?" He spoke with more confidence this time, the idea taking hold. "Edward is eighteen. He's got the training—"

"That, right there, proves what we're saying. God, Theo are you even listening to yourself? You'd rather drop everything and *leave* than face your past and the bullshit we're dealing with now. That's the height of avoidance issues." She moved around him and picked up her coffee mug. "Did last night mean anything? You said you want a baby, but how the hell am I supposed to take that seriously when you are talking like this?"

He hadn't forgotten. Of course he hadn't forgotten. He hadn't gone into last night planning to lay everything on the table, but now his words were real and so was the need to see Meg pregnant with their child. *Fuck.* He ran his hands over his face. "This has me messed up."

"Imagine that." Despite her sarcastic tone, she was

gentle when she wrapped her arms around him. "It's okay to be weak sometimes, Theo. It's okay not to have the answers. It's okay to lean on us. We lean on you often enough."

"When I'm actually there to lean on." Guilt threatened to choke him.

Meg squeezed him hard. "I know this might be shocking, Theo, but you're human. We're all human. That means we screw up sometimes."

She always did this. She could be as prickly as Galen, as prideful as Theo, but when they reached a breaking point, Meg was the one who held them together. She somehow always knew what to say to soothe the fractured bits of them, sanding the pieces down until they fit comfortably. It wouldn't be that easy this time but... It helped. He'd be lying if he said it didn't.

Theo rested his chin on her head and met Galen's gaze. "I miss him."

"I know." Galen picked up Theo's discarded mug and took a long drink. "He was a good man, and a good father." He stared down into the dark liquid. "I miss him too, Theo. It's not the same, but—"

"You were just as much son to him as me or Edward." It didn't matter to Theo's father that Galen was the son of a traitor. He'd only ever judged a person by their actions— never the people connected to them. It was part of what made him such a great man. Theo lifted one arm and motioned Galen closer, and then pulled him into the embrace, sandwiching Meg between them. They stood like that for a long time, and he let their arms around him lend the comfort he hadn't been able to ask for up to this point.

But eventually, the real world had to intrude.

Theo finally took a long breath and stepped back. "We need to talk about what happens tomorrow."

Meg hopped onto the counter and reclaimed her coffee, and Galen took up his normal spot leaning against the corner where he could see the entirety of the room. Theo poured a third cup of coffee and passed it to him, and then he had their full attention. He met each of their gazes in turn. "We know Dorian is involved, and we also know that Huxley is involved. Whether Noemi is or not—"

"She's not."

Theo shook his head. "Whether or not she has anything to do with your attack remains to be seen. We have to smoke them out, and the only way to do that is to make them think their plans are working so they'll make their move."

Understanding dawned in Meg's hazel eyes. "You want me to leave before they have a chance to escalate."

"I want you to give the *appearance* of leaving. Despite the evidence, you're safer within Thalania than anywhere else at this point. If we sent you back to New York there's a decent chance Dorian would see you as a loose end that needs to be tied up. Without the full protection our security can offer, you'd be vulnerable." He picked up his mug and set it back down without drinking. "You were hurt because we made a mistake and were too comfortable. I won't let that happen again."

Galen shifted. "Neither of us will."

"Okay." Meg tapped her finger against her mug, her gaze going distant. "What reason are you giving the Families for dragging them to the palace on such short notice?"

"Honestly? I was considering calling them out and seeing who reacted."

She shot him a look. "That's clumsy and you know it." Meg considered. "But what if... Okay, hear me out. Noemi doesn't want to be Consort. She wants to be Head of Family. Her father is planning on naming one of her male cousins."

"Probably so he can keep her free to slip into your shoes," Galen muttered.

Theo shook his head. "That might be part of it, but Huxley has never gone to its female descendants. It always passes from male to male." He had thoughts about that, but one of the key pieces of advice his father had drilled into him during his training was that they had to let the Families operate independently within their own power structures. As long as the scheming and backbiting didn't spill over to negatively affect Thalania as a whole, it wasn't the monarch's place to step in.

"Use this gathering to declare Noemi as Head of House. You'll rock the rest of them, and you'll earn her loyalty in one fell swoop, which will cut Huxley off from his power base—the Huxley Family. If he's out of favor that intensely, no one will touch him. Not even Dorian. And it might be enough to scare some of the people who were waffling on whether or not to support you into falling in line."

Galen snorted. "It doesn't work like that. He can't just wave a magic wand and meddle in Family business. It will backfire and then we'll have a rebellion on our hands in addition to whatever my father is brewing up."

"Wait." Theo lifted a hand, thinking hard. It wouldn't work exactly how Meg had proposed but... He closed his eyes, recalling the various bits of law that applied to this situation. He couldn't name Noemi Huxley the Head of Family, but... "If she makes the claim and usurps him, the Crown can support *that*. We can't step in with interior power struggles, but if she wins, we can ensure it's public knowledge that the Royal Triad supports her claim and looks favorably on the Huxley Family with Noemi at the helm."

Meg nodded. "Let me make a call." She hopped off the counter and padded out of the room.

"This is risky."

Theo nodded. "I know. We could be playing right into their hands."

"Don't see what other choice we have."

"Me, either."

A few minutes later, Meg was back. She gave them a particularly vicious smile. "Noemi's in. She's making her move today."

13

The second they were back in the palace, they scattered. Meg had her list of things, Theo needed to iron out some details about the gathering with the Families. Galen went in search of Kozlov. He found him exactly where he expected—in the head of security office. He shut the door and leaned against it. "If your little girlfriend fucks us, I'm going to skin her alive."

Kozlov barely glanced up from his monitor. "Good evening, Consort. What can I do for you?"

"Eyes on me, Kozlov."

He snapped to attention, just like he used to when Galen was head of security. *I could be again. Never would have dared hope for that shit, but here we are.* Galen moved away from the door and kept his voice low and even. "Noemi is making a play for Head of Family today. When the Families converge on us tomorrow morning, there will be chaos if she succeeds."

"She'll succeed."

Galen thought so, too. He'd never had a problem with Noemi leading up to this point. She'd been friends with Theo for a very long time, and she never tried to fuck him over the same way some of the other nobles had attempted from time to time. But she *was* a noble, and that made her untrustworthy. He'd spent too long living in his father's household not to understand how power bred contempt for anyone and everything less powerful. Noemi Huxley had been born into a charmed life, and having an asshole traitor of a father didn't change that fact. She might be offering a hand of friendship to Meg, she might even like Meg, but if Meg wasn't a Consort, Noemi wouldn't have given her the time of day.

They sure as fuck wouldn't have been holed up in Huxley's rooms watching movies the same way they had been the day before.

Even thinking about it, knowing exactly how vulnerable Meg had been, made him want to punch something.

He hadn't been able to indulge in that kind of destructive outlet for nearly twenty years. Ever since he'd come to the palace after his father's exile. Even with Theo's friendship, Galen had always been aware that he was one wrong move away from being turned out onto the street. Theo's father wouldn't have liked doing it—he was as good a man as a king could be—but he always put his country first. What did one life compare when it came to millions in the balance?

"Galen." Kozlov's deep voice dragged him out of the past. The giant of a man studied him. "Noemi has wanted Head of Family since she was a little girl, and she'll do anything to preserve her Family, especially if her father is a traitor. I know you don't trust her—it's not how you operate—but if she has the assurance of the King that she'll have royal support after she makes her move, she won't do anything to jeopardize that."

Kozlov's words told him all he needed to know. The man and Noemi had been fucking for years, but they were too good at keeping things under wraps in public for Galen to ever fully determine whether it was just a physical connection or if it went deeper.

If she'd told Kozlov about her plans... if he spoke about her with that tone of voice...

Yeah, the fool was head over heels in love with her.

"She'll leave you." Even as he spoke, he cursed himself for edging the conversation out of safer waters. But he liked Kozlov, and if the man didn't know what lay in wait for his relationship with Noemi, then someone had goddamn well better warn him. While Theo could do whatever the hell he pleased when it came to naming Consorts and giving the middle finger to tradition, the first female Head of Family for Huxley couldn't. Her enemies within the Family would be watching her every move, waiting for one misstep to cut her legs out from under her. Trying to be with someone like Isaac Kozlov—a man who was only half Thalanian and whose loyalty lay with the King and the King alone... They would crucify her.

Kozlov turned back to his computer. "She already has."

Well, fuck.

He shot a look at the door, but finally turned away from his escape route. "I'm sorry."

Kozlov sighed. "With all due respect, I don't want to talk about it." He pinched the bridge of his nose, took several deep breaths, and lifted his head. "Would you like to see the security plans for tomorrow?"

He could push for more, but Galen had never been all that good at comforting, and he'd no doubt fuck it up if Kozlov lost his mind and confessed his feelings. Better for both of them to keep this conversation safely in the professional realm going forward. "Yeah."

Kozlov cleared his throat. "You're sure about the circus today? It's a bold move."

He wasn't sure of anything anymore. Theo's plan hinged on so many moving parts that it made Galen's head hurt. He didn't like these kinds of games. The danger came from unknown factors and if it was just Galen... But it was never just Galen taking the risks. Theo and Meg would be right there alongside him, and they were arguably in more danger than he was.

He'd never felt so ineffectual in his entire fucking life, but Galen couldn't follow through on any of the things his instincts were screaming at him to do. He couldn't toss Theo and Meg into a van and haul ass away from this mess. It would still be there when they got back. Even if they *left* like Theo had talked about around this morning, trouble would just follow them. As long as Meg and Galen were alive and Theo was King of Thalania, Theo would be determined to keep them in the Consort position. If Theo *wasn't* king, it would be the exile all over again with his enemies needing him dead to ensure they remained in power.

No, there was no way out but through.

He had to trust that Theo knew what he was doing, had to trust the plan that depended on deceit and playacting, rather than hauling Huxley and Galen's old man into a room and punching until they got some answers.

He could do it.

He *would* fucking do it.

Galen met Kozlov's gaze steadily. "I'm sure. Show me the plans."

～

MEG CAREFULLY APPLIED makeup over her mostly-faded bruise. Her head still ached in the evenings, but that had as much to do with stress as with the putrid yellow color spiraling out from the side of her face. It'd be gone in another week or so. This conflict would be over by then, for better or worse. She looked over as the door opened and Theo walked in. He and Galen had been running around all day in hushed meeting after hushed meeting to get things set up for tonight, but they'd both been sending regular texts to update her.

She appreciated the effort.

Their time at Galen's place in Greece had ripped open wounds she'd barely been aware they were creating, leaving her feeling raw and exposed. In the past, that was when she'd lash out so she felt less vulnerable, but she couldn't do that now. She refused to. At some point, they all had to grow up and change the way they deal with hard shit. This just happened to be *her* moment.

She smiled at Theo. "Hey."

"Hey." He barely got a step into the room before the door opened again and Galen stalked in. He nodded at both of them and moved around Theo to the bedroom. His jacket hit the floor, quickly followed by his shirt, and despite seeing him shirtless more times than she could count, Meg stared.

"I brought something for you." Theo's amusement brought her back to herself, to the room. He hefted a garment bag over his shoulder, holding it easily despite it being in danger of trailing on the floor behind him. "I know you don't like gifts but—"

"Wait." She could feel Galen's attention sharpen on her as he sat on the bed, but she didn't look away from Theo. This small moment felt pivotal for reasons she couldn't quite put her finger on. Meg set down her makeup brush and stood to cross to him. "Show me."

Theo hadn't bought her clothes personally since the disastrous night when they had to flee New York. She hadn't appreciated it then, hadn't appreciated any part of that clusterfuck. But it brought her to this moment, to this relationship. Meg stopped in front of him and touched his face, running her finger along the sharp line of his jaw. "I haven't been particularly graceful about gifts, but I can do better."

Theo captured her hand and pressed a kiss to her palm. "Only if you want to."

So careful. Ever since their fight, he had been *so careful* with her. Meg wrapped her arms around herself as he moved away to hang the garment bag and unzip it. *No, not since the fight. Since the* other *thing.* "Do you really want kids?" she blurted.

Theo froze. She was pretty sure Galen ceased to breathe behind her.

She should stop while she was behind, but words bubbled up, pouring out of her mouth in a river she couldn't stop. "I'm not going to lie and say I've never thought about kids—even thought about kids with you guys—but it's all been theoretical and then you just throw that out there like it's a sure thing and..."

"I meant what I said." Theo spoke softly. Carefully. "It's ultimately your choice."

Yes...but no. It wasn't just her in this. She was one part of a triad. Since it would be *her* body doing the baby-making, of course she got the veto vote, but that didn't mean their opinions didn't matter. "Please answer the question. Do you want kids?" He glanced over her shoulder, and she tapped his chest. "Look at me, not him."

"Yes, princess. I want kids. My parents were the cornerstone of my life, and I want..." Theo ran his hand over his head. "I want kids. I want to be a dad. Even if I wasn't king, which requires heirs, I'd still want kids. I want a family."

She'd known. How could she not? But it had seemed such a distant theoretical concept.

It didn't seem the least bit theoretical now.

Meg kept her hand on Theo's chest and turned to Galen. "And you?"

"You already have my answer."

"I'd like it again." When they weren't all out of their minds from fucking.

Galen crossed his arms over his chest. "I have shit parents. I might be a shit dad." He looked at her and then at Theo, something tortured and painful sliding through his dark eyes. "With the two of you? It's selfish as fuck, but yeah, Meg, I want kids."

"I had such a terrible childhood." She didn't know if she was speaking to Galen or Theo, but they both moved. Theo slipped up behind her and wrapped his arms around her, cradling her with his body, lending her his strength. Galen closed the distance between them and did the same from the front. She inhaled deeply, letting their mixed scents wash over her. Here, in this safe space, she could give voice to the fear she'd kept wrapped in chains deep inside her for so long. "What if I'm just like her?"

"You're not." Theo kissed her temple. "You're strong and bold and fierce. There's nothing of her in you."

"Nothing except her DNA." Meg shuddered. All too easy to transpose herself over the memories of her mother. To taste the endless cigarettes coating her lips and throat with toxic smoke, to feel the cheap gin burning her stomach, to embrace the anger that churned deep inside her, to turn it outward at anything and everything under her control. "I'm already failing at so much. What if I fail at that, too?"

Galen gripped her chin and raised her face to meet his gaze. "Do you actually believe that?"

She started to say of course she believed that, but the weight of their bodies against her stopped her. That fear wasn't her reality. She'd fought so damn hard to ensure it would *never* be her reality. Did Meg actually think that she carried around some kind of time bomb in her genes that would explode the second she had a baby?

Ever since she was a kid, she'd carved her own way, had fought against the current that only seemed to travel to one destination. A future like her mother's. Even when she was eight, she knew she didn't want that. Did she really believe that a lifetime of choosing her own path would suddenly be worthless?

No.

"No," she forced out.

Galen nodded. "Then the only question remains is if *you* want kids."

It really wasn't much of an argument, after all. "Yes." In her heart of hearts, there had always been part of her that put children under the column of "someday." It had always just been a distant thought, a far-off plan. "Eventually, yes."

"There's no rush." Theo gave her a squeeze. "Whenever you're ready."

He might as well have told her that they *were* ready, but she appreciated the thought. Meg closed her eyes and let herself relax into their embrace. "Later. After we've gotten through this particular nightmare. After I finish my degree. Then..." God, she couldn't believe she was even saying this. "Then we can talk about having babies."

"Works for us." Galen pressed a quick kiss to her mouth

and moved away before she could sink into it. "Better check out the dress Theo picked for you before you hurt his feelings."

"Galen." The warning note in Theo's voice battled with something that might be joy.

She turned in his arms and, yeah, he was grinning like a fool. "You were really worried about that conversation."

"Yes." He gave one of those single shoulder shrugs. "I always knew where Galen stood on the subject, but your history meant you could fall on either side of that line. We hadn't talked about it."

They hadn't had any reason to talk about it. She shook her head. "You could have just asked me."

"I didn't want you to feel pressured."

Meg snorted. "Since when?"

"This is different. Children aren't like bedroom games or the power plays we make for entertainment. They aren't even part of the larger balance within Thalania."

He honestly believed that. Maybe it was even true. "They'd be part of it by virtue of their father...fathers? How the hell would that even work?" It had sounded sexy as hell —*scary* but definitely sexy—when he was staking his and Galen's claim on her in Greece, but the semantics didn't quite iron out so evenly.

"We wouldn't do a DNA test. I would simply formally adopt whatever children we have so that there's no contesting their claim to the throne."

"But that means that Galen isn't their legal father." She twisted to look at him, but he was merely watching this conversation play out as if he already knew how it ended and was impatient to get onto the next part. "Doesn't that bother you?"

"I could give a fuck what other people think. We have a

mostly equal relationship, and that's what will matter within the family unit." He made a face. "Though there's bound to be some noble having an apoplexy over the idea, or one of the distant Families thinking that they can use the 'problematic' genetic line to get a toe up in the power pyramid."

"They'll have to marry into the Families."

"Maybe."

Meg looked from Theo to Galen and back again. They'd obviously talked about this at length if they already had the future marriages of their *very* theoretical children planned out. "That seems like a shitty thing to demand just because we made the choices we did."

"It might be for naught." Theo gave another of his shrugs. "A lot can change in a few decades. Nothing is set in stone." He set her back a little and moved to put some distance between them. He almost always did that when he was about to put her on the spot. "You don't have to make a decision now. Or tomorrow. Or next year."

"Then you shouldn't have brought it up." Because she wouldn't be able to think of anything else.

"You're right."

The fact he didn't even argue or try to turn her statement around told her more than anything else put together. Theo really, *really* wanted kids. She wanted to tell him that of course they'd have a boatload of babies with dark hair, some with fathomless blue eyes and some with secret dark eyes. But when Meg opened her mouth, Theo pressed his fingers to her lips. "No, princess. Don't give us an answer right now, because you're going to give the one you know we want to hear. Take your time and think it over. There isn't a clock winding down on this one."

"Okay." The moment stretched out between the three of them, full with a future Meg suddenly wanted so badly, she could barely breathe past it. If she closed her eyes, she'd be able to see the life Theo wanted for them.

He'd be an overly indulgent dad, while simultaneously demanding that their children be their best selves, teaching them how to chase what they wanted while balancing it against the needs of their country. Galen? She could almost see him with a little girl on his knee, pretending to be put-upon to tell her one more story, but so blatantly wrapped around her little finger that Meg's heart actually leapt. And Meg? She pictured warm cuddles and laughter and a fierce protectiveness that took her breath away.

Theo might not want her answer yet, but she already knew what it would be. If she was perfectly honest with herself, she'd known the answer the second she decided to follow Theo into Thalania. He was king. A king required heirs, even in unconventional situations like theirs.

Speaking of...

"What would you have done if I said I didn't want kids?"

Theo considered her. "It would depend on the reasons and which part you're opposed to. If it's everything about pregnancy and children, then I'll pass the throne to Edward's children."

He would, too. There was no slyness on his face, no manipulations to ensure the outcome was one he wanted. He would honestly allow the throne to pass to his little brother's future children, rather than push Meg into a role she wasn't comfortable with. "I love you."

"I love you, too. Now, try on the dress. Everyone's arrived, and dinner starts in just over an hour."

14

Theo walked into the sitting room with Galen on one arm and Meg on the other. The former glowered at everyone in his impeccable tux, and the latter was resplendent in the violet gown he'd commissioned for her. With the expert makeup job she'd done, even he couldn't pick up traces of her bruise, and she carried herself as if floating on the ground. A trick she'd mastered somewhere along the way while he wasn't paying attention.

He wouldn't be so lax in the future. He'd missed things. Important things.

The invitation he'd sent Galen to deliver specified that the Head of Family was invited, as well as their heir. Theo let his attention drift around the large room and the people who'd gathered at his summons. Lady Nibley appeared to be sleeping, but she startled awake as he guided Meg into a chair near the fireplace. Lady Vann tried to subtly check out Meg's face, no doubt having heard the rumors of her injury, but when she caught Theo watching her, she turned her attention to her wine glass. The most notable addition to the room was none other than Noemi Huxley, sitting in a large chair on the other side of the fireplace, her cousin Wendy at standing at attention at her side. She'd formally filed the paperwork to be recognized as Head of Huxley a few hours ago, and the former Lord Huxley now occupied a space in a cell a few floors down where Kozlov no doubt had someone interviewing him.

Being part of an attack on the Consort was nothing less than treason, and the charges would be handled as such.

It was too much to hope that he could name everyone else involved in the process, but they hadn't been lucky up to this point. They were due a turn in their favor.

He couldn't afford to count on them getting it, though.

Theo nodded at Noemi and he and Galen took up positions on either side of Meg's chair. Custom dictated Theo was supposed to sit and his Consorts stand behind him, but with all the political players in the room, he felt better being on his feet and able to see the entirety of the room—including Meg. "Thank you for attending tonight."

Lady Nibley harrumphed. "Didn't give us much choice, did you?" She turned to Meg and leaned forward, peering up at her from beneath impressive gray brows. "You look well enough. Good for you. Don't let something as petty as assassins get you down."

"Grandmother," her heir hissed. "Show some respect."

"I'm ninety years old, pup. I don't have time to waste in the political dancing around." She met Theo's gaze. "You want to find the responsible parties. The Nibley Family will lend you any assistance you need to ensure that the traitors are found and brought to justice." A lengthy pause. "Assuming your word is good to bring my grandson back into the fold, of course."

"Of course." He'd known that was coming. No helping hand was offered without strings attached, Noemi and Lady

Nibley included. Since Theo had already decided that neither woman was likely to be involved in the attempt on Meg's life, he was inclined to meet their demands. This world was all about give and take, and their current situation was no different.

Lord Bakaj toyed with the stem of his wine glass, watching them with dark eyes. "We heard you had some trouble."

"Nothing we couldn't sort out," Theo responded easily. He looked around the room. All eyes had been on him—on all three of them—the second they walked through the door, but it was still a vital part of the dance to posture a little and wait for them to acknowledge he had their full attention. "The reason I requested your presence tonight is to formally recognize Noemi Huxley as the new Head of Family Huxley." New Head of Families were always welcomed officially by both the reigning monarch and the other six Head of Families.

All heads turned in Noemi's direction, and she inclined her head, as regal as a queen. If Theo hadn't considered her a friend for a good portion of his life, he might have missed the faint shadows lurking in her eyes. This might be a realization of her life's ambition, but it hadn't come without cost. He just hoped it was worth it.

"The formal acknowledgement will happen in the throne room after drinks." He forced a charming smile, knowing it looked natural even as it felt like it stretched his face like half-melted wax. There wasn't much to smile about at the moment, not with danger lurking so close. "Lords and ladies, please partake of my table and enjoy yourselves." Customary words to go with a customary situation.

Except there was nothing *customary* about this.

He didn't trust himself to touch Meg, to reassure all of

them that this was only pretend and enacting the plan they'd all put into place the day before. Appearances were everything, and they all had their roles to play.

With that in mind, he drifted toward Noemi. She looked particularly stunning tonight, dressed in a red couture gown that outshone nearly everyone in the room. *Not Meg. Not Galen.* But then, he was hardly an impartial party. Noemi saw him coming and gave him a bright smile. "Your Majesty."

"Come now, you know better than that. Theo. Always Theo." He took her offered hand and pressed a perfectly polite kiss to her knuckles. Theo forced his thumb to play over them before he released her. A tiny touch that would have gone unnoticed and unremarked upon if the room was occupied with any other group of people. "Congratulations."

"Thank you." Ever the politician, she kept her smile firmly in place, but her blue eyes flicked to Meg and back to him. "How is the Consort doing?"

"Galen's perfectly fine."

A tiny line appeared between her brows. "That's not the Consort I meant."

"Mmm." Every word dragged its claws through him, a betrayal that was only for show, but still felt so fucking *wrong*. It didn't matter how unnatural this was, that he would never *ever* pull a play like this normally, that Meg and Galen knew the truth. He wanted to call the whole thing off.

Impossible.

To back away now was to miss the chance to out their enemies, to put a stop to this insidious treason once and for all.

Theo raked his gaze over Noemi. "You look stunning tonight."

"Thank you." She shifted closer and lowered her voice. "I don't know what game you're playing at, but I want no part of it."

He reached up and tucked a stray strand of blond hair behind her ear. "Too late."

Heels clicking behind him might as well have been drums pounding out a call to battle. Noemi's eyes went wide and she stumbled back a step, and then Meg was there, gorgeous in her fury. "What the fuck is going on here, Theo?"

"Nothing," he replied smoothly. "I was just congratulating Noemi on her new position."

"Really? Because it sure as fuck looks like you're planning on doing a lot more than *congratulating* her."

Noemi held up her hands. "Consort, I can explain—"

"I don't want to hear it." Meg made a slashing motion and turned on him, hazel eyes blazing. "I put up with so much, Theo. So. Fucking. Much. And *this* is how you repay me?" She shook her head, looking sick to her stomach. "No. Hell no. I didn't sign up for this—for any of it. I'm out."

It took everything he had not to reach for her. Theo affected a bored look. "That's your call, Consort. No one is forcing you to stay."

"Yeah, I got that. Loud and clear." Her bottom lip quivered and she spun on her heel. Every eye in the room watched her disappear out the door, slamming it behind her hard enough to shake the walls.

Noemi made a move to go after her, but he caught her arm. "No."

"*No?* Are you out of your goddamn mind? She's your Consort," Noemi hissed, so low there was no way the words would carry. "You let her believe a lie."

He matched her volume and lowered his head, giving

the impression of an intimate conversation. "Leave it alone, Noemi. I have it under control."

Understanding dawned and her lips parted in shock. "You... I'm going to kick your ass to Istanbul and back when this is all over."

"When this is over, you'll have permission." He glanced over his shoulder to find Galen lounging in the chair Meg had abandoned. He'd poured himself a tumbler of bourbon and stared idly into the fire as if he wasn't fighting against the same need to chase down Meg now coursing through Theo's blood.

Lord Bakaj sent the door a significant look. "Do you need a moment?"

No going back now.

He smiled. "Not at all. Shall we move on to the throne room?"

MEG COULDN'T DRAW a full breath. She marched down the halls, not sure if anyone was watching her, but not willing to let her facade of anger wilt just in case. And, if she was perfectly honest, she *was* angry.

Theo and Noemi simply weren't the source.

How dare they make us jump through these hoops? We should be ironing out our life behind the scenes and moving forward into the future I can actually see, but instead we're playing games hoping to tempt someone into trying to murder me again.

Isaac Kozlov had an entire team of people watching her every move right now. There were cameras in most halls and rooms in the palace, so as long as she stayed out of the Families' wing, everything should be fine. Even if somehow she ended up there—not a choice she'd make lightly—they would know where she'd gone and react accordingly.

She just had to...

Footsteps echoed through the halls, mirroring her. Meg stopped short, but the sound didn't cease. She turned to find Alys hurrying toward her, trusty tablet in hand. The woman looked as exhausted as Meg felt, circles creating dark smudges beneath her eyes and her hair rumpled, rather than in its customary sleek ponytail. Even her clothes were slightly out of whack, her skirt wrinkled and her shirt buttoned up incorrectly.

Meg couldn't help wondering how much of her going MIA had to do with Alys unraveling before her eyes. The woman had her schedule and her routine, and Meg had blown it all to hell half a dozen times in the last week. It was no wonder she looked like a woman teetering on the edge.

Alys bobbed a little bow when she got close. "Consort."

"What can I do for you, Alys?"

"You shouldn't be out in the hallways alone, Consort. With the attacker still at large, it's important that you're with someone at all times."

She opened her mouth to inform Alys that she was fine, but Meg hesitated. "I'm just heading to get some coffee and then back to our private suites. The king and I had words, and I won't be attending the ceremony for Lady Huxley."

Now it was Alys's turn to hesitate. She clutched her tablet to her chest. "Is everything okay?"

Telling the truth wasn't an option. Theo had only brought in the select few people he trusted beyond a shadow of a doubt, and Alys didn't number among them. Meg liked the woman well enough, but that didn't mean anything in grand scheme of things.

She gave a shrug. "I don't know. I think he's going to replace me."

Did she imagine the sharpening interest in Alys's eyes?

She couldn't be sure.

The woman reached out and gave Meg's shoulder an awkward pat. "I'm sorry. He's always been changeable. You couldn't have known it wouldn't last." The movement dislodged her locket, and the silver necklace tumbled to the ground. "Oh, dear, the clasp has broken."

"I've got it." It was the least she could do. Meg bent over and scooped it up. The second her hand closed around the locket, she flinched. "Ouch. I think it might be broken. It pinched me."

"I've been meaning to get it fixed." Alys took the necklace back and slipped it into her pocket. "Thank you, Consort."

A wave of dizziness rolled through Meg. She swayed on her feet and pressed a hand to her forehead. "I... What?" *Focus. You have to focus.* But someone had switched out the solid floor beneath her feet for a ship on stormy seas. She reached for the wall to steady herself, and nearly fell when it was farther away than anticipated.

"Consort?"

"I'm fine." She most definitely *wasn't* fine. Another wave rolled through her, strong enough to make black dots dance across her vision. *Oh god, I'm going to pass out.*

"*Consort?*" And then Alys was there, slipping beneath her arm and hoisting her away from the wall. For such a small woman, she held surprising strength.

Meg tried to move with her, to stay on her feet, but she lost her heels within seconds and then faced the impossible task of navigating her gown. "Get Galen."

"I'm sorry, Consort. I truly am." Before she could process

that, Alys turned them toward the private suites. "We'll get you shaped up in no time."

Had she misread the regret in the other woman's voice? She didn't think so but... Nothing made sense right now. Meg tried to dig in her heels, to slow their forward motion, but the move made her palm twinge.

The same spot where the locket pinched her.

"You..." It took her three tries to put her words in some semblance of order. "You drugged me."

"A necessary evil, I'm afraid."

Meg tried to look up at the cameras stationed along the ceiling, but she couldn't do more than loll her head. "Help." The word emerged as a rasp, barely above a whisper.

"It won't make a difference. Right now, there's is a car crashing through the front gates of the palace and the security team is so distracted with that, they won't have noticed that the camera feed glitched the tiniest bit before starting a loop." Gone was the hesitant woman who hid behind her tablet and other people's schedules. The Alys holding her upright was as cold and impenetrable as an ice wall. A stranger.

An enemy.

Meg lot her ability to speak. Time fluctuated in time with her frantically beating heart, compressing when she most needed it to expand. Between one blink and the next, they'd left the halls of the palace behind and approached a set of doors Meg had never seen before.

Alys shouldered through, dragging Meg behind her. It spit them out into a secondary hall, which led to a loading dock. Meg let her weight go completely limp, though she couldn't say for certain if she'd done it intentionally or if the drug had finally taken her strength to walk along with her voice to cry for help.

If she thought that would slow Alys down, she was sorely mistaken. The woman barely paused long enough to haul her into a fireman's carry and then she kept going, hurrying to a car that had pulled up just out of the reach of the lights in the area.

One of the back doors opened and a large man emerged. For one breathless moment, relief nearly made Meg sick to her stomach.

Galen came. He's here. I'm safe.

But then the details hit her. His three-piece suit that he wore like a second skin. His jaw too refined. Silver at his temples.

Not Galen.

"Good evening, Consort." He smiled as Alys dumped her at his feet. "Allow me to introduce myself." He crouched down until he was at the same level where Meg sat, swaying place. "I'm Dorian Mikos, and I think you'll find we have a significant amount of things to discuss."

15

There was no sign of Meg as Galen followed the group of nobles down the hall to the throne room, but he hadn't really expected it. He slowed his pace, idly walking along and flipping through his phone as if he couldn't care less about the goings-on of this event.

It was the truth, albeit for different reasons than most of the attending people would expect.

None of them peeled off to follow Meg, but Galen hadn't really expected them to. In such a small gathering, a Head of Family or an heir coming up missing would be a giant smoking gun. He might not have a high opinion of nobles, but none of them were stupid enough to try something tonight.

No, they'd wait until they felt Theo's attention lay elsewhere, and *then* they'd move.

It meant keeping up the appearances of a fight for a while, maybe even for setting Meg up in different rooms, but they'd handle that as things fell out. In the meantime, Kozlov was interrogating Huxley, and his people were keeping an eye on Meg.

Galen's phone buzzed, and he stopped short. There wasn't a single goddamn reason for Kozlov to be calling him right now. He waited a few seconds, letting the group of nobles slip farther away, and then answered. "Yeah?"

"We have a problem."

Adrenaline kicked him in the stomach, but he forced himself to hold still, to not jump to conclusions. Kozlov was the head of security. A problem could be anything. It didn't have to mean Meg.

Yeah, he didn't believe that shit for a minute. "Tell me."

"I just got a call. Some asshole decided to ram the front gates. My men took care of him, but they didn't realize someone had slipped in a back door to the security system."

"*What?* That's not supposed to be possible."

"No shit. I don't know how they did it, but the fact remains that they *did* do it. I'm headed there now to ensure we shut them out. Do you know where the other Consort is?"

Galen's stomach dropped. "What the fuck do you mean, do I know where she is? You know the plan. Your people were supposed to be watching her."

"Fuck, fuck, *fuck*." He moved away from the phone, but his voice still came through the line clearly. "Find the Consort. Find her right fucking now and escort her back to the private suites, and get a goddamn detail on her." And then he was back. "Where are you? I'm coming."

Galen's thoughts went terrifyingly blank. They hadn't been lax in security tonight. It was the one night they *could* have extra people involved without raising any eyebrows since every single Head of Family was here. There should have been no damn way for Meg to disappear. He looked around. The group of nobles following Theo had turned the corner, but he could still hear them talking softly as they headed for the throne room. Meg had barely left ten minutes ago. She couldn't have gotten far. "No, fuck that. Go to the security hub and get our eyes up and going again. We can't find anyone if we can't see them. I'll start searching."

"Yes, sir. Keep your phone on you."

"Find her, Kozlov." He hung up and sprinted after the nobles. A breach in decorum, but Galen didn't give a fuck. Every instinct he had screamed that something had gone wrong, that they'd been outmaneuvered. That Meg was in danger and there wasn't a damn thing he could do to stop it. He bypassed the group easily and caught Theo's arm. "It's Meg."

Theo took him in between one breath and the next. His blue eyes went wide and he turned to the people behind him. "I'm sorry, but there's an emergency. We're going to have to reschedule."

Several people in the back of the group muttered, but Noemi stepped forward before anyone could really start shit. "Of course. Is there anything we can do to help?"

"Go back to your suites. There will be activity in the halls and the fewer people out, the better," Galen said.

More grumbling, but Noemi nodded. "I think it's time for a nightcap. Shall we?" She moved quickly, guiding the nobles away without seeming to herd them. A dangerous woman, to be sure, but she was in their corner so he had to be satisfied with that.

Theo barely waited for them to disappear to turn on Galen. "Tell me."

"Someone hacked the security cameras and set up a distraction so the team wouldn't realize they'd been put on a loop. We don't know where Meg is." Saying the words aloud made the whole situation that much realer. Meg was *gone*. Kozlov might not be sure of that fact, but Galen knew it beyond a shadow of a doubt. If he was more into woo-woo shit, he'd say the palace felt different without her in it, but that was impossible.

Her disappearing so quickly should have been impossible, too.

Theo closed his eyes and took a slow breath. "We're sure she didn't make it back to the suite?"

"Kozlov had a team check, but it was empty." Galen paced a tight circle. "They wouldn't have taken her through the front or out the side entrance. Too many people, even at this time of night. The risk of being seen would be too high."

Theo snapped his fingers. "The loading dock."

The only time anyone used that entrance was when they had shipments come in—or the staff snuck off for smoke breaks. Easy enough to time it right, a car driving up, someone ducking out, and then they'd be gone. Plus, it was actually the closest to their current position if a person went through the interior staff halls. Galen nodded. "Let's go."

They took off at a run.

Galen fished his phone from his pocket and dialed Kozlov. "Have your men checked the loading dock?"

"No. They were checking the most logical places and it didn't make the list." Kozlov cursed under his breath. "I'm working on getting the system purged now. I'll send some guys your way."

"Good." Galen hung up. He picked up his pace, edging out ahead of Theo. If they hit a dangerous situation, better for him to be the first one through the door.

"I didn't expect them to hit tonight." Despite nearly all-out sprinting, Theo was barely out of breath. But he had a wild look in his blue eyes that was twin to the panic pressing hard against Galen's chest.

"Neither did I." He shoved open the door to the kitchen and bolted through. "We fucked up."

Fewer than three minutes later, they hit the exterior door to the loading dock. Galen threw out a hand and stopped Theo short. "We go through slowly." Kozlov's men would be there at any minute, but charging into an unknown situation was a good way to get shot. It shouldn't have been a risk on palace grounds, but someone shouldn't have been able to snatch Meg and walk out, either.

They might not have proof that that's exactly what happened, but Galen knew it to be true.

Just like he knew that this situation had his old man's fingerprints all over it.

He edged through the door and then motioned Theo to follow. Even though part of him had hoped for different, they found the loading dock eerily empty. Theo cursed long and hard. "She's gone."

"We don't know that yet."

"She's gone, Galen. You know it, and I know it. Just like I know it's our fault."

A glint of metal against concrete caught his eye. He picked up one of the silver earrings Meg had worn earlier in the night. "We know she came this way." He was no tracker, but he still scoured the area, looking for signs.

Theo had his phone out. "Isaac? We know this is the way they got her out. Check the traffic cameras and see if you can narrow down the vehicle and a direction." He hung up.

Galen pocketed the earring. "It will take time for Kozlov to narrow down the results into something we can use."

"I know."

"You can't honestly expect us to sit on our hands in the meantime."

"I don't expect anything of the sort." Theo smoothed

back his hair and straightened his tux jacket. "We're going to interrogate the nobles."

FEAR morphed into fury with every step Theo took toward the room where the nobles had gathered for the second time that night. Whether or not the responsible party lay within the palace walls, they were *all* partially responsible for this nightmare.

So was he.

He stopped outside the door and turned to Galen. "Go to Kozlov and oversee things there. I'll call you when I'm done."

Galen's dark eye flicked to the door and back to Theo. "You sure you want to face them alone?"

"I have it handled." The worst had already come to pass. His actions, his place in the world, had put someone he loved directly in the line of danger. If they didn't move quickly... But no, that line of thought only ended in madness. He had to believe they'd recover Meg, had to believe that no permanent harm would be done to her, *had* to believe that they'd get through this just like they'd gotten through every other challenge up to this point. To do anything else would leave him on his knees and utterly useless.

Galen pulled him into a rough hug. "We'll get her back."

"I know." No time for doubt now. They had to move. "Go. I have this handled."

"Love you."

"Love you, too." He stood there and watched Galen walk away and allowed himself three beats of despair.

One. Meg was in danger.

Two. She might be hurting and scared.

Three. If they didn't pull this off, they might never see her again.

Fear washed over him in a crippling wave and he closed his eyes and embraced it. *Three. Two. One.* Theo opened his eyes and shoved every single feeling into a little box inside him. Deeper and deeper, until cold logic encased every part of him. He couldn't hold this distance indefinitely, but he could manage for the time required to accomplish this particular goal.

He walked through the door, every inch the King of Thalania. Lord Bakaj saw him first and moved to intercept. "What is the meaning of this?"

"Sit."

"You can't just—"

"*Sit.*" Theo turned his attention across the room. "All of you will sit down and you will listen. To do anything else is tantamount to treason."

They sat. Some of them—Lady Vann, Lord Popov— looked more nervous than others, but he could care less about their petty schemes and conniving bullshit. "I will ask you this once, and once only—who in this room has had contact with Dorian Mikos?"

Blanks stares from several of the nobles, shock from others. The only one who flinched was Lady Vann. Sickness threatened, but Theo held it at bay. He strode to her. "Where is he?"

"I don't know."

"Answer the question, Lady Vann."

She clutched her hands to her chest as if making herself into a smaller target would save her. "I don't see how it's any of your business."

"Dorian Mikos and his wife were convicted of treason

not once, but twice. Anything to do with them inside Thalania is my business." He towered over her, using his size to intimidate. "Tell me here or tell me in one of the interrogation rooms. It's your choice, Hollis."

Her whole body shuddered. "You shouldn't have brought that girl here. You shouldn't have tried to change things."

Lord Bakaj was the closest noble to her, and he took several large steps back, as if her treason was contagious. Theo barely spared him a glance. "This is the last time I'll ask nicely—where is he?"

She laughed, short and harsh. "I'm just one of the many players in this game, *Your Majesty*. Do you really think that there isn't anyone in this room who would pick up a knife if you turned your back? Don't be naive."

Theo turned a slow circle, meeting every set of eyes present. Lady Vann's heir looked sick to her stomach, but she would be investigated and tried on her own merits—or lack thereof—rather than on her mother's. Everyone else made an effort to hold their heads high and act innocent. Time would tell, but if the network was really as extensive as Lady Vann claimed, she wouldn't need to brag about it.

He strode to the door and leaned out long enough to motioned Isaac's two men forward. "Escort Lady Vann to the room next to Lord Huxley."

Everyone stood in silence as the screaming woman was dragged from the room. Theo gave them all one last long look. "If any of you have information about Dorian Mikos's whereabouts, coming forward now will result in a lenient punishment if my Consort is returned unharmed." No one moved. "If you have information and *don't* share it now, the truth will out eventually and the penalty will be death." A sentence of death for the crime of treason hadn't been used since his grandfather's time, but with Meg's life on the line, Theo wasn't capable of playing this carefully. He needed her safe, and he needed her safe now.

Silence reigned.

"So be it." He turned and left without another word.

Theo headed for the stairs leading down to where they kept the prisoners. He pulled out his phone and dialed Galen. The man barely had a chance to answer before he cut in. "Any news?"

"Nothing yet. Kozlov's got them out of the system, but they wiped the security feed for the fifteen minutes we need. He's doing the best he can, but it's not going to get us anywhere."

Damn it, he'd hoped there would be a simple solution for this. "Lady Vann is involved. I'm going to question her."

Silence. Finally, Galen took a deep breath. "Do you need me?"

Yes. He didn't say it. Galen had enough scars on both body and soul. Theo wouldn't add to them if he had any choice in the matter. Extracting information was the stuff of nightmares when it escalated past simple questions, but he was capable of doing it. His father ensured that he'd never give a command he wasn't capable of doing himself. Better for him to carry that price than anyone else. "I'm got it covered."

"Be safe."

There was no safety in this. Only danger and the kind of wounds that didn't weep blood. "Call if you find something."

"You, too."

Theo slipped his phone into his pocket and moved down the stairs. Once upon a time, there had been a true dungeon in the palace, but one of his distant ancestors had removed it during a restructuring overhaul of the building.

Prisoners and the like were relocated to a secondary location on the outskirts of Ranei, away from the general population and away from the nobles and their sensitive disposition.

He'd never found that change to be problematic. Until now.

A plain white room was too good for both Huxley and Vann. They had information he needed, and every minute they spent withholding it decreased the chance of Theo and Galen recovering Meg.

No, he couldn't think like that. They would get her back.

They had to.

He spotted the two men stationed outside the doors and strode to them. "O'Carroll. Bradshaw." Theo made a point of learning the names of those who staffed the palace regularly, and the habit paid off now. Both men offered him tight smiles.

O'Carroll was the elder, somewhere around his mid-forties, though he hadn't softened with age. He gave a short bow. "Your Majesty. We have Lady Vann secured to the table. What do you require?"

"Nothing for the moment." He slipped through the door and set eyes on Lady Vann. Her cuffs were looped through a metal ring in the center of the table, and the position left her slightly hunched forward. She tried and failed to look down her nose at him. Theo shut the door with a quiet click. "Lady Vann."

"You'll regret this, Theodore."

He smiled sadly. "You're under the mistaken impression that someone is coming to save you. Dorian isn't in the city. He took my Consort, and he left you to hang for it." He walked over and sank into the chair across from her. "You will, by the way. Hang, that is. We're not equipped for an electric chair, and I've always found it rather inhumane. Though I suppose that's part of what made it such an attractive option. People are less likely to commit killing offenses if they think they might be strapped down and hooked up to a machine meant to fry their brain."

She blinked big brown eyes at him. Fear finally slithered through their depths. "Exile is the punishment for treason."

"Exile *was* the punishment for treason. Unfortunately for you, it's no longer quite the deterrent it used to be. You, my dear, are to be an example to all who come after." He sat back and considered her. "I suppose I could have someone rig up a guillotine. It worked for the French."

"That's not funny."

"Who's laughing?" He shrugged. "I don't have all night, Hollis. Either tell me what I need to know or tell me who has the information I need to know. Those are your options, full stop."

"You'll really kill me. *Me.* Lady Vann. Head of the Vann Family.'"

Theo lowered his voice, a confidence between just the two of them. "I would happily execute you and every other Head of Family if it meant my Meg would be returned safely. All seven of your lives don't begin to measure against hers. Yours alone? Don't make me laugh." He reached over and covered her shaking hands with his. "Tell me where Dorian's taken her."

"What's to stop you from killing me if I do?"

"Nothing. You're the villain of this piece, but I have no problem picking up the mantle in the meantime. Final chance, Hollis, or I go next door and talk to Huxley. He might not be a main player in the game, but I wager he knows enough to give me a direction."

She gave a laugh, but not like anything was funny.

"Dorian is in Williamshire." A small estate in Vann territory that edged up against the border of Greece.

Theo was already moving. He shoved out of his chair, ignoring Hollis's demand for assurances, and charged out of the room. He had his phone to his ear as he took the stairs two at a time. "Galen, she's in Williamshire. Meet me on the roof."

16

Waves of painful awareness crashed through Meg, pulling her out of the darkness. Her body had morphed to a strange combination of concrete and taffy while she was out, the drug leaving everything dull and impossible to extract herself from. She lay perfectly still and tried to figure out where the hell she was. The last thing she remembered...

Alys.

Dorian.

Did Theo and Galen know she was gone yet? She had no idea how long she'd been out, but surely she wouldn't go missing in the freaking palace for more than thirty minutes without *someone* noticing. No, they had to know she was gone by now.

"Good morning, Consort."

She dragged her eyes open and squinted into the bright light of the room. It was empty except for the cot she lay on and the chair occupied by Dorian. Meg stared at him for a long moment, and then slowly pushed herself up into a sitting position. She doubted her legs could hold her at this point, but having a conversation with the enemy while she was on her back was out of the question. Another glance around the room offered no clues to where they'd taken her.

Dorian gave her a warm smile, the kind meant to be reassuring, but all it accomplished was sending alarm bells blazing through her. "I think it's time you and I had a little talk."

"Why?" She pressed a hand to her forehead. Everything hurt, but her head most of all. It throbbed in time with her heart, the pain somehow bigger than her skull. "Why keep me alive? It's obvious you want me out of the palace. Why bother going through this song and dance and wasting everyone's time?"

He chuckled. "I can see why my son likes you."

He's not your son anymore. She bit the words back. Antagonizing him wasn't a smart idea, no matter how much she wanted to throw sentences at him like swords, to try to deal him even a portion of the pain he'd dealt Galen over the years. Instead, she did her best to swallow down her anger and focus. "We have a lot in common."

"A unique kind of fire." He leaned forward and braced his elbows on his thighs. "From a trailer park to the palace in Thalania. I have to say, your ambition outshines even my own. It's rather impressive."

It's not like that. I didn't plan on this. More words, stuffed down deep. Meg leaned carefully back against the wall the cot had been shoved against. The room kept spinning, and the last thing she wanted was to collapse and reveal just how screwed up the drugs still had her. She was in no shape to make a run for it. Even if she was physically capable of it, she didn't know where she was, what the layout of this place looked like. She needed more information, and the only current source of information was smiling at her like he'd just won the lottery.

Whether it was the Mega Millions or Shirley Jackson's Lottery depended solely on Meg.

"You have a point. Get to it before I puke on your shoes."

"Mmm. I should apologize about the drugs. Alys gets a little over-excited at times and she wasn't sure she could convince you to follow along without a little... assistance."

"Lovely." She'd never particularly liked Alys, but Meg had always chalked that up to what the woman represented —an ever-present reminder that Meg would never be good enough, would always be stepping in some kind of mess every time she left her suite. She had ignored her instinctive dislike because she blamed herself.

Way to go, Meg. The enemy was right under your nose and you had no idea.

Dorian shifted. "You're obviously a woman who knows her worth, and knows how to make the world work for her."

Would he say that if he saw her staggering student loans? Or how close she'd been to going under completely before Theo and Galen walked into her life? Meg was resourceful, sure, but that sort of thing only went so far. Sometimes the world just kicked a person in the teeth and kept on kicking until they were curled in a ball, helpless on the floor. Meeting Theo and Galen was nothing short of chance, and everything that had happened since sometimes felt like the best kind of fever dream. Up until recently, Meg had taken no ownership of that, but she wasn't about to admit as much to *this* man.

When she didn't immediately jump in, his smile widened. "I think we can help each other."

She laughed. She couldn't help it. "I'm sorry, but do you

usually try to kill people before you recruit them? Doesn't seem like the most effective policy."

"Ah. Yes, well." Dorian grimaced. It was the tiniest of breaks in his smile, but present all the same. "Plans change and, as I mentioned, Alys is... overzealous."

So Alys *had* been the one to shove her down the stairs. Meg suspected as much after the whole poisoning incident, but she tucked the confirmation away for later use. She pressed her palm to her forehead. The dizzy spells weren't abating, and though she'd mostly threatened to puke on Dorian out of spite, it might be a very real possibility in the near future. "Why don't you stop pussyfooting around and tell me what you're offering?"

Another low chuckle. She hated that he almost sounded like Galen when he laughed like that, loathed even the tiniest of similarities beyond their blatantly shared physical traits. He straightened. "You want to stay in the palace. I want to ensure my goals are enacted by the Crown. Like I said, I think we can help each other."

Clarity sifted through her, slower than she would have liked. "You want me to, what, be your mole?" Meg frowned. That didn't make sense. He had to know she had absolutely no incentive to do what he wanted. "Why?"

"You're uniquely positioned." Dorian examined his palms. "I think I've made it quite clear I can get to you—and anyone in the palace—if I want to."

"You have," she said slowly. "But I'm already here. If you're going to kill me—"

"Oh no, my dear. Not you." He looked up, the warm seeping from his expression, revealing the snake beneath. "But it would be increasingly unfortunate if people around you simply began dropping like flies. Poison is such nasty business, and so easy to administer. Maybe to a shiny new

Head of House. Or perhaps to a certain princess who meddles in things she had no business interfering with. Or even the King himself. The possibilities are truly endless."

Meg stared. Was he really planning on blackmailing her with the safety of the people around her? Devious, to be sure, but... It still didn't make sense. If that was his play and he was just as brilliant and everyone seemed to think, he would have gone about it in a different way. "So you're just going to take my word for it and let me go if I agree to this?"

"The consequences for you breaking your word are high enough to warrant consideration."

They were, but... Meg shook her head, the room giving another sick turn around her. Something was wrong. Something... She exhaled harshly. Dorian wanted her dead. That was the one consistent factor that ran through this whole nightmare. She'd done nothing in that time to make him think it was possible to turn her, and he wasn't a stupid man. Evil, yes. But not stupid. He had to know she would go directly back to Galen and Theo and tell them everything.

Then why not murder her here and now? Why not take her out while she was still drugged and just dump her body somewhere? *That* was more logical than this weird blackmail situation. The only thing he offered by allowing her a chance to get back to Theo and Galen was...

Hope.

He offered hope.

What better way to hurt someone than to give them a moment when they were sure everything would be fine, and then snatch it away at the last moment? Meg closed her eyes, but that only made her dizziness worse. "Will it be a sniper set up to take me out the second I'm within touching distance of them? You can't let me get back into the palace and the relative safety it offers. Another accident won't work now that everyone's guard is up, and you burned Alys's cover when you had her take me." The words tasted foul on her tongue, but realizations hit her, one after another. What had he mentioned... "Poison. It's got to be poison. How long will I have? A day? A week?"

She opened her eyes to find him appraising her with new interest in those dark eyes. He pushed slowly to his feet, towering over her, but made no move to come closer. "Smart little thing, aren't you? Brave and foolish like my son. Cunning like Theodore. No wonder they couldn't resist you."

"I won't do it. I won't go back just to hurt them."

Dorian shrugged and headed for the door. "It doesn't really matter what you think, my dear. You are just a pawn in a larger game. My boy had a chance to return to the fold and chose not to come to heel. Now he'll be brought to his knees as everything about him turns to ash. Starting with you." He walked out of the room and closed the door softly. The sound of the lock clicking into place echoed through Meg's head, making everything hurt more.

Time. I just need time. He brought me here for a reason instead of just having Alys dose me. I have time, and it's not over until I'm dead.

She slipped back to the cot and rolled carefully onto her back. She just had to think. To plan.

There was a way out of this. She just had to find it.

GALEN STARED through the binoculars at the house on the cliff. "Going to be tough." They stood on the boat they'd rented earlier today from a town several miles away.

"Walk me through it." Theo's voice curled through the

space between them, a comfort and a glaring reminder of their missing piece.

Galen took a deep breath and told him what they'd discovered up to this point. Maybe Dorian had started in Williamshire, but he'd left right around the time they got surveillance up, traveling to his place in Greece. They'd followed covertly, and, for all intents and purposes, he appeared to have settled in here.

Satellite images told them that storming the house by land was damn near impossible. It was even tougher to get to than Galen's place, and he'd intentionally purchased that house for its location and natural defenses. Only one narrow road approached his old man's house, and there were snipers set up on the hills on either side of it. In fact, judging from the heat signatures, he had an entire team around the house.

Which was why they were here, dressed in knitted sweaters and boat shoes and with every single female member of Kozlov's security team draped around the boat in tight clothing and making a show of drinking themselves stupid. It might be off season for this kind of thing, but idiot rich men had been partying on the Aegean since time began. The security staff would note their existence, but as long as they acted the part, that's all they'd do.

He expected his old man was otherwise occupied.

No. Can't think about that right now.

"What if she's—" Theo's thoughts had obviously shadowed his down that dark path.

"She's alive. If he wanted her dead, better to do it in the palace and prove how ineffectual we are." He hated how quickly his mind grasped his father's intentions, even after decades of avoiding the man. Dorian was always scheming, always looking for a toe up and an opportunity to kick out the legs of the people around him. He had a plan in place when he'd taken Meg, and something so simple as death at his hands wouldn't satisfy it. "I'll bring her back, Theo."

"I know." Theo cleared his throat. "You come back safely, too."

"I will." Another promise he couldn't guarantee that he'd keep. He finally looked at Theo, at the worry written across every line of his face. "Thank you for staying in the boat."

Theo made a face. "I'm no use to you up there. Isaac's team is better trained and they've worked together for years. You can slip into that dynamic without an issue, but I can't." He ran his hand through his hair. "But that doesn't mean I have to like it."

"I know." They walked down below deck to where Kozlov had laid out the plans for the house and now stared at them as if he could divine their secrets. "Best guess, she's in the basement."

"Makes sense." Less chance of an escape that way. Galen surveyed the plans and the map surrounding them, filled with markers to indicate where the patrols were. Galen and Theo took seats on the other side of the minuscule table. "We come up this way." Galen touched the cliff face next to the docks. Dorian had two men on the docks themselves, and another two covering the narrow staircase up the cliff to the house. He really only needed two men since it bottle-necked too effectively for a swarming attack.

They weren't going to swarm.

They were going to scale that fucking cliff and take out everyone who got in their way. Galen clenched his fists. "We go as soon as it's dark."

"Yes."

One of Kozlov's people guided their ship away from the

house, keeping up the meandering path of a part-time sailor with more money than skill. It wouldn't do them any favors to bring attention their way or cause anyone in that house to ask questions that would raise suspicions.

The hours passed slowly and too quickly, all at once. They went over the plan again and again, until Galen practically vibrated with the need to move, to act, to do something other than sit in this too-tiny space filled with emotions he had no answer for. Going out on deck wouldn't be any better, and he'd end up tracking the sun in the sky and calculating the distance left to travel.

For once, Theo offered no distraction. He simply sat in silence, his thoughts likely occupying the same dark space. Without looking over, he laced his fingers through Galen's. "We *will* get her back."

"Yes." Meg believed in the power of words and actions, and if they couldn't act in this moment, they still had their words. "We'll get her back," he confirmed.

Theo nodded and went back to watching the light glint off the water outside their boat.

Time passed, the seconds solidifying into minutes, minutes hardening into hours. As the last sliver of sun sank beneath the horizon, the low sound of a motor cut through the silence. Kozlov pushed to his feet, though his height required him to bend to avoid knocking his head on the ceiling. "It's time."

MEG WOKE FEELING… not refreshed. Nowhere near refreshed. But when she opened her eyes, she felt a little less like death. The room no longer spun and her headache had decreased into something just shy of tolerable. She lay still for several long minutes, counting her inhales and doing her best to calm the thoughts racing in circles through her mind.

She had no idea where she was.

She had no idea what the building looked like outside of this little room.

She had no idea how she was going to escape, or what she'd face if she was able to.

The only thing she knew was that she had to try.

One last inhale and she pushed slowly up to a sitting position. When the room stayed firmly in place, she stood. *So far, so good.* She walked carefully around her room, examining it from every angle, letting her legs get used to pulling their weight again. The space was exactly what she'd seen the first time. Four white walls. A cot welded to the floor. No windows to speak of.

And no bathroom.

Good.

Meg let weariness wash over her. She'd never been an actress, but she'd have to pull that skillset out of her ass right now. It didn't take much playing pretend to shamble back to the door and insert hoarse panic into her voice. "Hey! Hey, I need to use the bathroom."

"Hold it." A gruff male voice that most certainly wasn't Dorian.

Thank god.

She hit the door again, harder. "I just got my period. I can't *hold it*. It's going to look like a murder happened in here if I don't get some feminine products *and* a bathroom. Now!" Meg held her breath. This kind of ploy would never work on a guy who was the least bit familiar with how menstruation worked, but she'd wager Dorian didn't hire his men for their feminist mentalities.

Sure enough, a low curse sounded on the other side of the door. "Back away and sit on the bed. I'm coming in."

"Thank you. Oh god, *thank you*." She obeyed the command, but she cupped between her legs for good measure, as if she really was terrified about bleeding out on the floor. "Please hurry."

The door opened mere seconds later, but she counted three separate clicks before it did. *Taking no chances there.* She couldn't let them put her back in this room. She'd never be able to escape if she stayed locked up here. She wasn't sure she *could* escape, but she'd damn well try.

The man who walked through the door looked like he'd been pulled from a casting lineup for Nameless Mercenary #2. He had tattoos peeking above the collar of his shirt and his muscles bulged out from beneath a black T-shirt that was at least two sizes too small. Fatigues and shiny black boots finished off the look. He even had a scar through one of his eyebrows, a perfectly straight shiny white line that almost looked fake.

He looked around as if expecting to be doused in blood at any moment. "Come on. Don't... get it anywhere."

"I'm trying." She kept her hands strategically placed and followed him out of the room and into a narrow hall. If Meg had Galen's skills, she could have pulled some fancy move and incapacitated the man—or maybe just punched him into unconsciousness—but all she had was herself. She shuffled along behind him, doing her best to take in everything without looking like she was doing exactly that.

They turned one corner and then another, until he all but shoved her into a bathroom. "There should be something in there. Hurry up." He slammed the door in her face.

Meg wasted no time. She rifled through the cabinet for something useful, but it only held the usual things. Manly razors. Shaving cream. A handful of toothbrushes and two types of toothpaste. She eyed the bar of soap in the shower. Maybe she could embed the razors into it and use it as a slashing weapon? She'd seen it done in a movie once but...

No, it might work against one person, but she couldn't fight her way out of this place with that kind of weapon. She hadn't seen a weapon on her guard, so there was no guarantee he had a gun, and...

Stop. Breathe. Focus.

She used the toilet and then made a show of rattling around and making pained noises after she was finished. Her gaze lifted to the tiny window positioned near the ceiling. It was too narrow for a grown man, but Meg could probably wiggle through. She sure as hell had the motivation. She just needed the time.

"Hey! Hurry up in there."

She jumped. Time was one thing she *didn't* have. Yet. Meg pasted the most pitiful look on her face and cracked open the door. "There's nothing in here, and the toilet paper is so thin, I'll bleed through it inside of an hour, even if I layer up. Should I do that?" *Come on*, she silently urged. *You don't want to have to drag me to the bathroom once an hour until Dorian decides to enact his evil plan.*

The same thoughts must have been dragging through her guard's mind because he gave her a disgusted look. "Stay in there. I think the upstairs bathroom has something." He took a step back and looked at her, his dark eyes soulless. "I mean it, little girl. Stay the fuck in that room if you know what's good for you. I might be nice, but the rest of my team isn't, and if they find you out alone..." He shrugged. "You won't like it."

Great. Good to know. She let her bottom lip quiver. "I won't go anywhere."

"Better not."

She shut the door and counted slowly to five, long enough for his heavy footsteps to move away from the bathroom. This was the only chance she'd get. Meg threw herself into motion. She climbed onto the back of the toilet and worked the latch of the window loose. It unlocked without a sound and she muscled it open.

Salty sea air drifted into the bathroom, as familiar as her own name. No telling how far they were from the ocean, but at least she had a starting point. Meg cast one last glance over her shoulder and hauled herself up and through the window. It was a tighter squeeze than she liked, and she had to wiggle to dislodge her hips from the opening, but the fact it was so close to the ground worked in her favor and she was able to claw herself free. She carefully closed the window and crouched in the shadows, trying to get her bearings. The house blocked what little moonlight the night sky offered, and all that lay before her was darkness. In the distance, she thought she caught the soft sound of water, but she couldn't be sure of that. Maybe her nose was making her ears play tricks on her.

No telling which direction was the right one. The only thing she knew was that she couldn't stay here. The guard would be back in a few minutes—if not less time—and then she'd be in trouble.

She was already in trouble.

Meg counted slowly to three and pushed away from the house. She had to *move*. Rocks cut into her bare feet, and she had to hold her dress off the ground to prevent it from dragging. Evening gowns were hardly created for stealth. She reached a waist-high rock ledge and paused. She *knew* these rocks. Well, not these specific ones, but this type.

Greece.

She was in Greece.

She squinted into the dark. The ledge stair-stepped up into the night, probably to some kind of cliff face. At least that's what the land around Galen's house did. If Dorian's was set up in similar fashion, there would only be two ways out—a road or the water. She looked both ways, but in the end there was really only one option. Any route that allowed cars in and out would be watched *much* closer than the way down to the sea. She had no idea what she'd do if she managed to *get* to the water. Summer was many long months away, and a cruel wind bit through the flimsy fabric of her dress. Swimming meant a nasty case of hypothermia.

If she didn't drown first.

Can't think about that now.

She edged in the direction she was now *sure* she could hear water sounds from. Maybe they weren't as high up as Galen's place was. Maybe it was just a matter of getting to the water, to a dock, and stealing a boat. Meg had never actually hotwired anything before, but she'd give it her best shot.

Several agonizing minutes later, the rock ledge she'd followed fell away into emptiness. She caught sight of a couple bobbing lights that might have been buoys or boats far, far below her. *Damn it.*

"Someone's been naughty."

The voice skittered up her spine and she spun as a man shifted away from where he must have been standing this entire time, watching her make her slow progress. His teeth flashed in the low light, but that's the only impression she got of him.

That and *danger*.

Meg took a step back, but he was too fast. He grabbed her arm and yanked her roughly enough that if his body hadn't been there to stop her forward momentum, she would have fallen. "Pretty little thing, aren't you? No wonder Mikos kept you locked up tight away from the wolves." His grin made her skin want to detach from her body and flee into the night. "Should have stayed where he put you."

"Let go of me." She shoved at his chest, but he was too strong. "I'll—"

"Scream?" He laughed. "Yeah, I don't think so."

Meg kicked at him, but her bare feet did more damage to her toes than to his boots. It didn't matter as he dragged her farther from the minuscule light emanating from the house. In desperation, she went for his eyes, scratching and trying to dig her thumbs in the way one of the lady self-defense classes her college had offered last year.

He cursed and released her long enough to raise his arm to backhand her. Meg threw her hands over her face. *Oh god, this is going to hurt. Don't pass out. Don't you* dare *pass out.*

The blow never landed.

The man's hold on her was gone so quickly, Meg stumbled. She hit her knees and dropped her hands in time to see his limp body disappear into the darkness. And then she was pulled against a large male chest. Instinct had her fighting, but then his scent hit her. Beneath the salt smell of water was a hint of cloves and tobacco.

Galen.

17

G alen allowed himself to hold Meg for a beat. Two. On the third, he smoothed a hand over her hair. "Can you stand on your own, baby? I need to cut this dress down to size and get you the fuck out of here." Galen had run countless scenarios on how this night would play out, and not a single damn one of them had included finding one of the guards grappling with Meg out in the dark, away from the house. And yet here she was, whole and shaking, but relatively unharmed.

He hoped.

He went to his knees and pulled the knife from the sheath in his boot. He sawed through the dress just above Meg's knees and then yanked it away from her body. It was too cold for her to be dressed like this, but better to have her legs exposed than to trip and fall down the narrow staircase carved into the side of the cliff.

Or to bring attention to them.

He cupped her face with his hands. Even in the low light, he could see black tracks down her face where she'd shed tears. It made him want to march into that house and put a bullet between his old man's eyes. Not now. Not tonight. Tonight, they only priority was getting Meg home safely. After... Well, they'd worry about that shit after the fact. "Can you walk?"

"Yes." She leaned into his touch, seeming to soak him in as much as he soaked her in. "Let's get the hell out of here."

"Took the words right out of my mouth." He considered his options and grabbed her hand. "Stay behind me until we get to the stairs, and then you're going to go first." He and Kozlov's team had already taken care of the guards in that area. The last target had been the one with his hands all over Meg, and he wouldn't be bothering anyone ever again.

She nodded. "Okay."

"You got this far. Let me take it the rest of the way." He drew his gun from his shoulder holster and guided them into the darkness. There wasn't anywhere to hide, the rock barren around them in a way that had to be designed. He knew, because he'd done the same with his place. Galen hated seeing physical evidence of how similar he and his father's minds worked, but there was no denying it. He actually approved of the security measures.

The only thing his old man didn't count on was Galen himself.

Two women melted out of the darkness and he recognized them as Zara and Alexis from Kozlov's team. They fell into formation behind him as if they'd done this drill a thousand times. "Clear," Zara murmured. "They have shift changes in seven minutes, so we need to move."

"We have less time than that." However Meg had escaped—and they'd be talking about *that* later—they were bound to notice sooner, rather than later. "Let's get the fuck out of here."

As if on cue, someone started shouting at the front of the

house. Galen tightened his grip on Meg's hand and pushed her in front of him. "Down the stairs. Now." He pointed at Zara and Alexis. "Cover our retreat, but you stick to me, you hear me?"

"We don't answer to you," Alexis narrowed her eyes in the direction of the house.

"What she means to say is 'Yes, sir!'" Zara checked her rifle and nodded. "Go. We're right behind you."

He went. His priority was Meg. He had to trust that Kozlov had trained these women well enough. That *Galen* had trained Kozlov well enough.

He shadowed Meg's steps, keeping one hand free in case he needed to pull her back from the edge, but she never faltered. Down and down and down they went, the shouts and curses above them gaining volume. "Almost there, baby. You're doing great."

They reached the dock just as shots rang out above them. Galen grabbed Meg to him and twisted to keep his body between her and any bullets headed their way. Alexis and Zara returned fire and he rushed Meg to the boat. It was a tactical boat barely big enough to hold the four of them. He and the women had to paddle it in to avoid detection, but it would get them out of here in a hurry. He dumped Meg into it and turned to find Zara next to him. Alexis was still on the stairs, firing up at the men crowding the top of the staircase, her laugh a wild thing on the wind.

Goddamn it.

He pointed at Zara. "Cover me."

"You can't—"

But Galen didn't give a fuck what he couldn't do. He charged up the dock and grabbed Alexis around the waist. She cursed, but kept firing as he walked them backward down the last few stairs and across the dock. He dumped her onto the boat next to Meg. Zara didn't wait for him to toss her in. She leaped gracefully down, and then it was Galen's turn.

Zara worked the motor and he pulled Meg into his arms, using his body to shield the worst of the wind. Galen looked up just as a man came to stand at the top of the stairs, his familiar form backlit by the lights of the house. Dorian. He watched them as Zara got the motor started. He watched them as they sped away from the dock, bullets peppering the water around them. He watched them until Galen could no longer make him out, until the house itself was just a smudge in the distance.

Alexis ripped open a package and shook out a blanket. "Here, Consort."

He considered calling her out on the stunt on the stairs, but he wasn't head of security. Yet. Instead, Galen wrapped the blanket around Meg and held her closer. Shakes racked her body, and he couldn't tell if it was fear or adrenaline let down or the cold. He didn't know what to say, so he kept it simple. "You're safe. I've got you. You're safe." Over and over again as they sped across the surface of the Aegean Sea.

～

You're safe. *I've got you.*

Meg clung to Galen and waited for her body and mind to accept that truth. Part of her feared she was already halfway gone, delirious with drugs and hallucinating in the basement of Dorian's home. The other part? Down deep, where hope couldn't touch it, she feared that Dorian had wanted *this* all along. Her escape. A rescue. A glimpse of safety before whatever poison he'd dosed her with worked its evil magic and swept her away from Theo and Galen for good.

Say something.

You can to say something.

You can't offer him false hope.

Meg clutched Galen's shirt. "Poison."

"What?"

She had to lift her voice to be heard over the waves. "He might have poisoned me. That was his plan. I... I don't know if he already did it while I was unconscious."

Galen's grip on her spasmed, but his face fell into its customary expressionless mask. He kept one arm around her and dug a phone out of his pocket. "Theo, get the helicopter ready. We're on our way." A pause. "Have the doctor on standby as soon as we touch down at the palace." His dark eyes drank in the sight of her. "I don't know if she's okay. Just... Just have the shit ready, okay?" He hung up.

"That was cruel."

"Telling him you're okay when you could start vomiting blood or something fucked like that is cruel." He gathered her back to his chest, the feel of him wrapped around her smaller body creating a lie that she was safe. "Try to relax."

"What if they come after us?"

"They won't."

As if it was as simple as that. "But what if they do?"

Galen cursed, low and rough. "Then I'll put a fucking bullet in their brains. You're not going back there, Meg. Not ever. You're safe, and if the bastard poisoned you, then we'll get a goddamn antidote and un-poison you. You're our happily ever after, and this isn't one of those fucked up love stories you like to watch where someone dies at the end." His voice broke, just a little. "Sit here and let me hold you and know that you're safe."

The truth washed over her. As terrified as she'd been, as helpless and at a loss... Galen had been, too. And Theo, as well, no doubt. She slipped her arms beneath his jacket and hugged him close. He was *shaking*. "I'm okay. You got to me in time."

"I might not have."

Meg shifted closer yet, pressing her face against his throat. Finally she lifted her head. "You did."

If he was Theo, he would have spent another ten minutes kicking himself, maybe a day or two beyond that brooding over everything that could have gone wrong. Theo *would* do that once he was sure she'd survived mostly intact. Galen simply took her words as truth and nodded. "You're right. I did."

Meg glanced at the two formidable women sitting on the other side of the boat. One manned the motor, steering them with a determined look in her dark eyes. The other stroked her rifle as if it was some kind of pet and kept her head on a pivot, searching for some sign of their enemies.

She must have fallen asleep at some point, because the next thing she knew, a rough bump of the boat jarred her into waking. Meg opened her eyes just as Galen stood and lifted her with him. He stepped onto something far more solid than the boat—the dock—and then Theo was there, pulling them both roughly into his arms.

Things happened quickly after that. A frantic trip to the waiting helicopter, and a tense few hours' ride back to the palace. Through it all, Theo and Galen never let go of her. They also didn't say a single word. Their presence comforted Meg, even as it woke the awful feeling that nothing would ever be okay again. What would happen to them if she died the way Dorian planned? Would they become shadows of themselves? Would they keep going with only the slightest hitch?

No, the latter was her insecurity talking. They loved her. If Meg was sure of nothing else, she was sure of that.

She tightened her grip on their hands. "Don't let him win. If... If I'm poisoned, don't you *dare* let him win. Take your time. Grieve. But then you find someone else. Don't let this be a fissure that damages you irreparably."

Galen's jaw went tight, but it was Theo who barked out a rough laugh. "No, princess. You're not going to fade gracefully into the sweet embrace of death while handing out fortune cookie advice. In fact, you're not going to do it at all if I have anything to say about it." He brought her hand to his lips and pressed a kiss to her knuckles. "We're almost there."

A dizzying descent brought them to the roof of the palace. A flight of stairs, two turns, and they walked into a part of the building Meg had never been in before. She looked in askance at Theo, but it was Galen who answered. "Staff quarters." He opened a door, leading the way into what appeared to be a hastily thrown together hospital room.

Dr. Oakes greeted her with a warm smile. "Welcome back, Consort." His gaze flicked to Theo and Galen and then back to her. "Are you well enough to change? We have some tests we need to do."

The last thing she wanted to do was get into a sterile hospital gown and submit to being poked and prodded, but Meg nodded. They had to know if she'd been poisoned, and they had to know now. It had been hours since her escape, and though she didn't feel any worse for wear, other than the nasty headache and vague nausea that had plagued her from the moment she woke up, they had to know. They just had to. "Okay."

And so it began.

After reentering the room, Dr. Oakes took vials and vials of blood, which he carefully handed over to a nurse who disappeared immediately, probably to start testing it. Then, with comforting words and gentle hands, he examined every inch of her body, asking her careful questions all the while.

No, she hadn't eaten anything.

No, she wasn't assaulted to the best of her knowledge.

No, she wasn't aware of anything being administered, with the exception of the drug that knocked her out to begin with.

In the end, it was over far more quickly than she expected. He sat down across from her and gave her a serious look. "I can't find any needle marks, except for the one on your palm. They could have potentially hidden a secondary one there, though, so we will check your blood again. But your vitals are all fine and though you'll be feeling the effects of the drug for a little while, you seem to be otherwise unharmed."

Something like hope coiled through her. "You mean maybe he didn't get a chance to drug me."

"I mean that I'm going to run some tests on your blood, but most poisons I'm aware of that could be administered in a way that he could have managed without you remembering are ones that would act fast—within a few minutes or a few hours. We're past that window at this point." He held up a hand. "It's possible there's still something left to find, but if I were a betting man, I would bet that you slipped out of there before he had a chance to put things into motion."

"When will we know for sure?"

"Soon. One way or another, we'll know soon." He pushed slowly to his feet. "I'm going to let those boys in here, but if they get you too worked up, they have to leave."

The doctor might be on the far side of sixty and kinder than most people she'd met, but she didn't doubt for a second he could kick both Theo and Galen out of the room if he decided it was in her best interest. Meg managed a smile. "Okay. We'll behave."

"See that you do." And then he was gone, quickly replaced by Theo and Galen. With their energy taking up too much space, the room suddenly felt three sizes smaller. It *should* have dredge up feelings of claustrophobia, but Meg wanted to wrap the sensation of their presence around her like the warmest of blankets. Here, in this tiny room, for the first time in what felt like days on end, she felt truly safe.

Through some unspoken agreement, they took up spots on either side of her and each laced his fingers through hers. Meg took her first full breath in what felt like years. "Dr. Oakes thinks I might be okay."

"He told us." Theo ran his finger over her knuckles again and again and again. "How do you feel?"

Nothing less than the truth would do. "I'm freaked out. Every time I close my eyes, I see the look on his face or feel that guard's hands on me or..." Meg shuddered. "If Galen hadn't shown up when he did..."

"Then you would have kicked his ass down the cliffs." Galen's rough voice soothed something inside her, as if he firmly believed his words. As if he hadn't seen just how helpless she'd been, how firmly ruled by panic.

"I want self-defense lessons. I know we talked about it before, but I want them now. And I need to brush up on my shooting." She was more than passably good with a rifle thanks to her upbringing, and shotguns took barely any skill at all, but handguns were something else entirely. She knew enough to not shoot someone—or herself—on accident, but that was the sum of her experience.

Galen exhaled long and slow, as if doing that would keep his first response in. Finally, he said, "Will that make you feel more in control?"

"Yes." Irrational, but she wasn't prepared to set aside her fear yet. She didn't know if she even could.

"Okay. Then we start Monday."

Theo kept up that constant stroking, his touch an anchor she allowed to settle through her. He spoke softly and clearly. "You're safe, Meg. You're here and you're safe, and we'll never let anything like that happen again."

Maybe it wasn't a promise he could make, but she let him make it all the same. Meg relaxed into them, letting their big bodies buoy hers, letting their strength bolster her up until she no longer felt in danger of coming apart at the seams. "As long as Dorian's alive, he won't stop. He's too determined to make Galen hurt—to make both of you hurt."

"Let us worry about Dorian, princess. He won't come near you again."

He had no business promising that, and she had no business believing it, but when Theo spoke, the truth seemed to spill from his mouth. It was some strange combination of confidence and pure privilege, but staring up into his blue, blue eyes, Meg actually believed him. "I love you. Both of you."

"We love you, too."

Suddenly, she couldn't get the words out fast enough. "I want this. I know I said it before, but I want this, full stop. I still want to finish my degree, but I want you and you and I want babies and all the bullshit with the nobles and Thalania. I want *us*."

"How do you feel about a fall wedding?"

Meg blinked. "What?"

Theo studied her left hand and stroked over her ring finger. "Make this official in a way that has nothing to do with Thalania." He shifted, sliding off the bed and coming down on one knee in front of them. "Marry me, Meg." He raised her left hand to his lips, and then claimed Galen's left hand and did the same, pressing a soft kiss to his ring finger. "Marry me, Galen."

The list of reasons why it was impossible ran nearly as long as her arm. Meg simply didn't give a fuck. She wanted this. She wanted it forever, and she wanted it for always. "Yes." She turned and looked at Galen. "Marry us, Galen."

His dark eyes jumped from one of them to the other, raw and filled with a longing he rarely let through his careful control. "You're serious."

Theo held his gaze steadily. "I've never been more serious."

Galen looked at Meg. "You do this, there's no taking it back or changing your mind. It's us—the three of us —forever."

She let him see exactly how much this meant to her—to them—and repeated, "Marry us, Galen."

"Goddamn it, like I'm going to say no." He pulled them forward into a kiss. It was messy and complicated and perfect. "Yes. Yes, I'll marry you. Yes to a fucking fall wedding or spring wedding or whatever the fuck you want. Just *yes*."

∼

Three weeks later

Theo walked into his hotel room and carefully locked the door behind him. He'd known who was waiting for him the moment he left the ring shop earlier, but he'd taken the circuitous route back. Time enough to have a quick phone call with Meg, to check in with Galen and assure him that Theo was not, in fact, taking foolish risks on his first trip out of Thalania since Meg's attack.

Now, he flipped on the light and smiled. "Dorian. Strange coincidence, finding you in my hotel room."

The dark-haired man pointed a gun at him. "You froze my accounts."

"Did I?" Theo shrugged and tossed his bag onto the coffee table. "Seems to me that you've gotten into bed with powerful people who have terrible track records. It could have just as easily been one of them that decided to teach you a lesson."

Dorian visibly shook, his face going red and angry. "Don't fuck around with me, you little shit. My wife left me. Disappeared. *Everyone* has left me. Call that goon of yours, Kozlov, and instruct him to release the holds on my accounts. Then, if you're lucky, I won't shoot you where you stand."

Theo reached for his phone. He drew the gun nestled at the small of his back in a smooth move and fired two shots into Dorian's chest. Before the other man realized what had happened, Theo stalked to him and knocked his gun away. Dorian's eyes went wide. "You shot me."

"Yes, I did." Theo gripped his arms and guided him to the floor and leaned him against the wall. He sat back long enough to send a quick text to Isaac. *It's done.*

Dorian rasped a wet laugh. "My boy will never forgive

you for this. He might hate me, but he'll..." He coughed. "He'll never forgive you."

"You're a fool, Dorian." Theo smoothed back his dark hair, so similar to Galen's. "You'll never have a chance to hurt those I love again. And your body will never be found." He pushed to his feet and went to answer the knock on the door. Isaac and a trio of people walked into the room.

Isaac took one look at the dying man on the floor and gave a short not. "You should have done him slower."

"Probably." Theo looked at Dorian and waited for guilt to flare or something akin to regret. It never came. The only thing he felt was a vicious satisfaction that he'd taken the necessary steps to ensure the man never came near Galen or Meg again. Without that driving force sowing dissent in the Thalanian ranks, they finally had a chance at peace. "Let's finish this up, Isaac. I want to go home."

EPILOGUE

"If you try to put Theodore Fitzcharles IV on his birth certificate, I will gut you."

Theo braced himself against the back of the bed and held perfectly still as Meg did her best to break every bone in his fingers. When the contraction ended and she slumped against his chest, he exhaled carefully. "What name would you like?"

"You're humoring me, and I hate that you're humoring me." He'd braided her hair back from her face as soon as they realized the contractions weren't slowing down, and he was glad for that fact now. They were both straining and sweating, and the last thing she needed was to worry about hair in her face. Meg pointed at Galen where he paced the space in front of the bed. "Stop that. You're making me nervous."

"Should it be taking this long?" Galen ran his hands over his head, his eyes too wide. "I'm going to go get that goddamn doctor and get some answers."

"Galen." Theo put enough snap in his voice to stop his husband. "If you piss off Meg, she's going to gut *you*. Dr.

Oakes has things well in hand. The baby is in position. He just stepped out of the room for two minutes. Breathe."

Someone in this room had to breathe, because it sure as hell wasn't going to be Theo. He'd attended birthing classes with Meg, had read all the books, had educated himself on everything pregnancy and baby related until he drove both her and Galen up the wall.

None of it had prepared him for the experience of Meg going into labor. Of the pain that turned her body into a tight spasming ball of fury that he could do nothing to abate. He had her supported with his body, had given her something to cling to, but it didn't seem to make a difference when each new contraction hit. She cursed, she squeezed his hands to mush, she threatened the kind of violence that would have been impressive under different circumstances. Through it all, he could only endure. That was his only role in this—to do whatever she needed.

Another contraction hit and Meg let loose a breathless curse. "God, that one really hurts."

Galen went wild-eyed. "That's enough right fucking there." He charged to the door and threw it open.

Dr. Oakes stood there, his brows raised. "Do you need to take a walk, Consort?"

"No," Galen growled.

"Then stop with the theatrics." The doctor motioned his nurse into the room and then moved with purpose to the end of the bed and gave Meg a kind smile. "Breathe, yes just like that, I know it hurts, Consort, but you're doing wonderfully." His presence took the tension in the room down several notches. Once the contraction passed, he pulled his chair closer. "I'm going to check your cervix."

Several seconds passed.

Dr. Oakes took a careful breath. "Looks like your little

fellow's been busy. It's time." He jerked his chin at Galen. "Consort, if you would help brace her knee while she pushes. Nurse Lecanter, if you could take the other knee." He met Meg's gaze. "When the next contraction comes, I need you to bear down and push. You're going to meet your son soon."

"Okay." Meg panted, each breath tearing at Theo's control. "Okay, I can do this."

"You can do this," he murmured in her ear. "You are strong and powerful and our child is lucky to have you as a mother. You're almost there, princess. We've got you."

Just like that, it was time. Theo breathed with her, Galen held her leg, his expression at once panicked and rapturous. It was happening. She was having their baby. Holy fuck, Theo hadn't expected this level of emotion curdling in his chest. Fear and joy and hope. And he could do nothing but wait for the conclusion, whispering an endless string of comforting words to ground Meg as she fought to bring their son into the world.

"Good, good." Dr. Oakes smiled. "He's crowned. Another couple of pushes and he'll be here."

So it went. Time lost meaning. There was only contractions and brief respites. All color had leeched from Galen's face, and Theo imagined he looked just as terrified. *Should it be taking this long?* He couldn't voice the question, couldn't do anything to bring fear into this room. Dr. Oakes had things well in hand. He *had* to.

"There we go."

A shrill scream sounded through the room and Theo's heart actually stopped when he realized it hadn't come from any of them. No, it was... the baby. Dr. Oakes let loose a little laugh. "Well, apparently your son isn't a son at all." He lifted the tiny baby. "Congratulations on your daughter."

Things happened quickly after that. Galen cut the cord, the doctor dealt with the afterbirth, their daughter was delivered to Meg's bare chest, and both were wrapped in comfortable blankets. He and Galen ended up on either side of her, staring down at this tiny person that they'd made. She looked much like an angry old woman, but she was still the most beautiful thing Theo had ever seen. He stroked the side of her sleeping face with a single finger.

"Louise," Meg whispered. "I want to name her Louise."

Theo would have given her the world in that moment if she'd asked, but he hesitated. "Are you sure?" Louise had been his mother's middle name and while he loved the idea of honoring her this way, he'd been serious when he promised Meg that she could pick any name she wanted for their child.

"It's a good name," Galen said, his voice hoarse. He smoothed a careful hand over Louise's head. "Fuck, she's perfect."

"She really is." Theo turned his head and kissed Meg's temple. "I love you. Both of you."

"Love you, too." She sounded half asleep. "Would you like to hold her?"

"Yes." He carefully took Louise and arranged her against his bare chest like the nurse had shown them. Theo covered her back with a careful hand, delighting in the slow and steady rise and fall of her breathing. A baby. They had *a baby.*

His life had been full of major highs and devastating lows, and this moment, right here, was the worth the entire ride. He pressed a soft kiss to Louise's crown of dark hair. She had a full head of it, which delighted him to no end. "Your life comes with great privilege, little girl, and great responsibility. You are our jewel and our treasure and we will protect you to our dying breath. Our family is a little unconventional, but you will want for nothing. You will spend your life surrounded by an abundance of love."

"Forever," Meg said.

Galen gave a shaky grin, his dark eyes shining in the low light. "Always."

AFTERWORD

Thank you so much for reading THEIRS EVER AFTER! I hope you enjoyed the conclusion of Theo, Galen, and Meg's story as much as I enjoyed writing it. They really are something special!

If you enjoyed the book, please consider leaving a review.

Want to stay up to date on my new releases and get exclusive content? Sign up for my newsletter!

COMING SOON!

Isaac and Noemi's story, THEIR SECOND CHANCE, will be released on audiobook through the Read Me Romance podcast from December 10th-14th. You can listen for FREE!

If audiobooks aren't your thing, you can find THEIR SECONDS CHANCE on all retailers in Spring 2019! The ebook will also feature exclusive bonus content.

THE MARRIAGE CONTRACT

New York Times and *USA Today* bestselling author Katee Robert begins a smoking-hot new series about the O'Malley family—wealthy, powerful, dangerous, and seething with scandal.

The Marriage Contract

Teague O'Malley hates pretty much everything associated with his family's name. And when his father orders him to marry Callista Sheridan to create a "business" alliance, Teague's ready to tell his dad exactly where he can stuff his millions. But then Teague actually meets his new fiancée, sees the bruises on her neck and the fight still left in her big blue eyes, and he decides he will do everything in his power to protect her.

Everyone knows the O'Malleys have a dangerous reputation. But Callie wasn't aware of just what that meant until she saw Teague, the embodiment of lethal grace and coiled power. His slightest touch sizzles through her. The closer they get, though, the more trouble they're in. Because Callie's keeping a dark secret—and what Teague doesn't know could get him killed.

Find out more in <u>The Marriage Contract</u>. Out Now!

To stay up to date on new releases and for exclusive new content, make sure to join Katee's newsletter <u>HERE</u>